# BROKEN PROMISES

Kenneth's eyes narrowed. "What, may I ask, were you doing with him in the first place?"

"What I should have been doing with *you*—walking in Hyde Park—had you come to see me as you had promised!"

She felt his arm stiffen around her, then relax. "I am sorry. Sometimes I don't know—I feel—" He shook his head and smiled down at her. "Well, I promise I'll do better, Aimee. I swear it. You will forgive me, won't you?"

Kenneth looked suddenly as he had when they first met, carefree, with a laughing glint in his eyes. Her heart beat harder—if only he would look at her like that more often!

He smiled and brought her hand to his lips. "Do you still like promises, Aimee? I remember you did . . . a long time ago."

He said it as if it had been a hundred years past. *It has been that long,* cried something in Aimee that ached terribly. But she smiled and said, "Yes . . ."

# Cupid's Darts

*Karen Harbaugh*

A SIGNET BOOK

SIGNET
Published by the Penguin Group
Penguin Putnam Inc., 375 Hudson Street,
New York, New York 10014, U.S.A.
Penguin Books Ltd, 27 Wrights Lane,
London W8 5TZ, England
Penguin Books Australia Ltd,
Ringwood, Victoria, Australia
Penguin Books Canada Ltd, 10 Alcorn Avenue,
Toronto, Ontario, Canada M4V 3B2
Penguin Books (N.Z.) Ltd, 182-190 Wairau Road,
Auckland 10, New Zealand

Penguin Books Ltd, Registered Offices:
Harmondsworth, Middlesex, England

First published by Signet, an imprint of Dutton Signet,
a member of Penguin Putnam Inc.

First Printing, February, 1998
10 9 8 7 6 5 4 3 2 1

 REGISTERED TRADEMARK—MARCA REGISTRADA

Printed in the United States of America

# Prologue

Lieutenant Kenneth Hathaway felt the sudden tang of spit upon his tongue and tightly closed his teeth, gritty with dust . . . or the anticipation of battle. His heart beat faster, and his skin pricked with sweat as he shifted his body uneasily upon his horse. He squinted into the sun and then glanced at the faces of the men he would lead into the fight. If what he himself felt did not show on their faces, he knew them well enough to know they felt it, too, at least in part. For him, it was always like this before combat, an exquisite twist of hot excitement and fear. Now he was to fight on the hilly plains near Salamanca: a sea of red earth, the color anticipating the spill of blood to come.

He did not regret joining the army, though his father had fought hard against this ambition; Kenneth, too, had found the glories of war not so glorious. But it was for a good cause, and his men were good men, and he could wish for no better leader than General Lord Wellington. There could be no nobler cause than to fight against the Bonaparte beast and for the safety of his country and its allies.

A ripple went through the lines, and a sharp shock of emotion went through him. They would engage the enemy soon. He smiled grimly, and noticed a lightening of the expressions on his men's faces when they looked at him. They saw his smile and took hope from it; they did not know it was hysteria—and hysteria it was, he was honest enough to admit, though he'd never tell them so—that would soon seize him and make him laugh like a madman once he began to fight.

Beserker. That was what one of his men had called him; the man remembered tales of the wild Viking warriors and told them from time to time. The wildness had come upon Kenneth since a boy, and he'd always known the army was for him—where else was such a thing useful? And so he had joined, against his father's wishes.

He looked up. The signal came, and with a shout he thrust his heels into his horse's sides.

The roar of men's voices and the thunder of horses' hooves against the earth rose up around his ears. The sound pulsed into him, pressing painfully upon him. He leaned forward in his saddle. His horse went faster. As he charged into the enemy lines, his sword upraised, the pressure within him burst in the pit of his stomach—and he laughed.

He laughed as his sword bit into the enemy before him. A French foot soldier stared at him in terror and ran.

"Mad Hathaway's at it again!" cried one man at his side.

"Then we're sure to win this one," called another.

But he heard their voices as if in a fog, far away, for he was caught up in the rise and fall of his sword, the movement of his horse beneath him, and the thunderous waves of men and guns. It went on and on—he did not know for how long. Hours, perhaps, for after a while the beserker force had run its course and the smile on his lips had turned into a grimace of determination. His arms ached, his legs burned, and he could feel the labored breathing of his horse beneath him. The sun beat upon him and sweat trickled down his leg—or blood, for his thigh pained him. He glanced around him.

The dirt was red with blood, darker than the rust-colored earth, and the bodies of men and horses were strewn upon it. He swallowed, then cursed his distraction as he deflected a blow at his ribs.

He was in a dangerous state. The battle was not yet over, but he was weary and too conscious of the destruction around him. His mouth was dry, but there would be no time to take a drink from his water bag. His eyes momentarily caught a familiar profile upon the ground—was it Lieutenant Connelly?

A bright flash of steel caught his eye. He brought his arm up in time to catch the slash of a saber upon the guard of his sword and turn it away from his face. He could not think of friends lost, not now.

His gut ached—he felt drained. He needed something . . . something to spur him on. He thought of Lord Wellington and his heartening words before the battle, but remembered also the bleakness in his eyes—the general well knew that destruction would come with battle. It always did.

What of his men who trusted him? Kenneth did not know how many he'd led to their deaths. Weariness crept over him and the next swipe of a French sword slit the sleeve of his uniform. Kenneth raised his sword and slashed in return, his movements mechanical, without thought.

"Remember me. . . ."

The soft sweet voice slipped from his memory into his ear, and awoke other memories. Bright summer sun, the scent of musky grass, the cool breeze of his own sweet England. . . .

And the deep blue eyes and soft sweet smile of Aimee.

Aimee, whose kisses and quick embraces were shy, her whole manner pure and innocent. His own Aimee, who'd pleaded with him to come home safe, so they could be married at last.

"Aimee . . ." he whispered.

New strength surged through his body and joy sang through his blood. He spurred his horse forward with a shout and a wave of his sword. Behind him, he could hear the cheers of his men and he grinned fiercely.

*This* was what he fought for—for cool green fields and skies as blue as Aimee's eyes; lovely Aimee, shy Aimee. Aimee, whose hair was the pale gold of England's sun, not the harsh brass of Spain's. Aimee, the embodiment of all his dreams of England, pure and sweet.

"Aimee," he murmured as he fought and rode and plunged forward into the thick of battle. "Aimee," he said as he parried and thrust and slashed. "Aimee," he cried as he brought down one enemy soldier after another.

Word spread through the French ranks of a mad Englishman who smiled and spoke of love as he wreaked terrible death around him. He was possessed of a demon, surely, and they fled before him, for nothing could defeat an unnatural creature like that.

Lieutenant Hathaway awoke the next morning and ran immediately to retch outside his tent. The memories of blood and death from the day before were blurred, for which he was thankful, But the memory of last night was also blurred, and he knew he shouldn't have drunk the bottle of captured French brandy, however much his men insisted he celebrate the victory with them and drown the grief for friends lost. He was not one to drink of spirits much, and it had gone to his head immediately.

Sweat broke out on his forehead and he heaved again. God, he was a mess. He crawled back to his tent and found his progress impeded by a mass of fabric. Weakly, he rose up on his knees.

It was a woman. A camp follower, perhaps, although her face was pretty and delicately made. But she was sunburned and her hands callused and rough. She snored gently. He could smell brandy on her . . . or perhaps it was on himself.

"Remember me . . ."

Aimee's voice floated through his mind and guilt seized his gut, making him feel even more ill. The memory of his betrothed's words and face had brought him through death and into victory—and what had he done?

He had profaned her trust in him. Or had he? He looked down at his clothes and saw he'd slept in his uniform. A few of his buttons were missing, his shirt pulled out from his trousers, but he was not in enough disarray that he could have done much, if anything, with the woman. He closed his eyes and made himself remember—no, he hadn't. He vaguely remembered the young woman weeping and fainting with fatigue—she had lost someone, and he had felt sorry for her. Francis Pargeter had taken her away . . . but how had she come here? Perhaps she had wandered here in the night? It was easy enough to do—the tents looked much alike in the dark.

A wave of dizziness hit him and he groaned. But whatever the case, the sooner he got the woman out of his tent, the better. He wouldn't want word of this to get back to Aimee. Not that he'd done anything wrong. Kenneth groaned again. It hurt to think. It was best not to think at all, just *do*.

She was, thank God, not very heavy. Not that it mattered. He could hardly keep on his feet as it was, and his thigh wound, though slight, hurt badly enough so that he sucked in a quick breath as he lifted her. A surge of relief went through him—there! He couldn't have done anything, not with that thigh wound. But where to put her? He gazed blearily around the camp, then spied a particularly neat and tidy tent. He grinned, then winced as pain shot through his temple. He waited a moment until the headache and dizziness receded to a dull ache, then reeled in the direction of the tent. Lieutenant "Priss" Pargeter-Hathaway—the most dandified and fastidious man in the brigade—would wake up to an interesting surprise. Not surprise . . . she'd gone with him in the first place, hadn't she? Kenneth closed his eyes briefly again at the ache in his head and frowned.

He didn't like Pargeter. The man was next in line for the baronetcy, and even though he was not a true Hathaway, he dared presume to use the Hathaway name in conjunction with his own. Not in front of Kenneth, of course, but he'd heard about it from his friends. A damned insulting presumption.

Kenneth did not know how he managed to deposit the woman next to Pargeter without waking them both, but he did. He never cared much for the man even though he was a cousin many times removed. Kenneth could hardly bring himself to acknowledge the connection, for the man irritated him, caring more for the state of his clothes than for the men under his orders. He wondered what "Priss's" reaction would be to the woman in the tent. Any man— not betrothed or married, that is—would succumb to temptation, but Pargeter was either extraordinarily discreet or as active as a eunuch as far as that went. Perhaps the presence of a pretty young camp follower might make him reveal his ways. Kenneth closed his eyes, feeling as if someone were pounding with a hammer from just behind his eyes. He was thinking too much again.

He turned to leave the tent and was struck again with dizzying nausea. He ran out of the tent and retched again.

God help him, he would never celebrate a victory in this way again. It was not worth it.

The image of Aimee floated before him, and he felt ashamed. His inebriation and having that woman in his tent . . . it made him less than worthy of his betrothed. Unless someone put the woman in his tent . . . not that it made things much better. He wove his way back inside the tent. A glance at the mirror nailed to a tent post made him shudder. Damn, but he looked worse than the devil. Definitely not worthy of Aimee. Seizing a pail of water, he drank from it and then poured the rest of it over his head.

The shock of the water cleared his mind a little. Tea— he wanted tea. He closed his eyes and remembered how Aimee poured tea into delicate china cups, and how her hand curved just so around the cup as she drank. He sighed. All he'd get, though, was coffee. It would do.

Lieutenant Hathaway straightened his clothes the best he could and went in search of Sergeant Jackson, his batman. If he had to have coffee, Jackson was the one to make it—good and strong, the best antidote for a lieutenant bent on being worthy of the loveliest, the most virtuous of women . . . Aimee Mattingly.

If someone could have seen the youth who descended to the camp, they would have thought he was just another fresh-faced, albeit very well-favored young soldier not much above the age of seventeen. Except, of course, for the fact that he did not wear a uniform and descended not from a hill or even a tree, but from the sky . . . and he had wings. He carried a roll of cloth under his arm and a quiver of arrows on his back, as well.

However, Eros was careful not to let anyone see him, although it took a great deal of energy to keep himself invisible. This place of war was not his place, it was Ares's,

the antithesis of all that Eros was, and so it drained him.
But he had promised Psyche Hathaway, Kenneth's sister,
that he'd watch over her brother and help keep him safe.
Eros sighed. He felt tired after yesterday's battle, and had
borrowed a young ensign's uniform just in case he could
not keep up his invisibility. He frowned as he put on the
clothes, and made his wings disappear as he put on the
shirt. It was becoming more and more difficult as the
years went by to maintain his godly powers. He had
found it almost impossible in this war camp to conjure up
a uniform and decided to borrow one instead. Perhaps
that was the price he had to pay for being in a place of
war, or perhaps for staying earthbound for so long. But it
was necessary until his quest was done.

However, the uniform fit, and he fancied he looked
quite well in it, although it restricted his movements more
than his usual chiton. He looked around and heard some
retching noises. He grinned. It must be Lieutenant Hathaway. He had spotted Kenneth as he descended and had
seen his hasty exit from his tent.

He frowned as he watched Kenneth bring a woman out
of his tent and take her into another man's. What was
this? He had sensed something quite different from Lieutenant Hathaway during the battle, an almost holy love
for his betrothed, Aimee Mattingly. It had driven him to
fight more fiercely than before and had even given Eros
increased energy, enough to produce the arrows of repul-
sion that he shot into the French soldiers in front of the
lieutenant. And now there was this woman whom he'd
apparently taken to his tent.

Of course, it did not mean Hathaway was in any way
enamored of the woman. However, he remembered all
the jokes he'd heard from the men around him, about
how Kenneth "hath a way" with the ladies. Normally, he
would have ignored them, but Psyche did say that she

wished him to watch over Kenneth's welfare and he did wish to please her in this. She was his friend, after all, the only one on this mortal world.

Perhaps he should ensure that Hathaway stayed faithful. Eros bit his lip in frustration. Miss Mattingly was not here, however, and this would make increasing Kenneth's attachment to her more difficult. Perhaps a portrait would work. He moved silently into Hathaway's tent and waited until the man left it.

Eros rummaged around in various bags until a round metal object touched his hand. Ah! He pulled it out and there it was—a miniature painting of Aimee Mattingly. He looked at it critically. It idealized her features, making her seem more perfect than she really was. Her face was a little more heart-shaped than the perfect oval shown, and her nose not quite as straight. Her hair was a deeper gold than the portrait's, and her eyes not as blue. The portrait was chillingly beautiful; Aimee, he recalled, was warmly pretty.

But it was close enough in resemblance that it should work. He placed it in a prominent place in the tent, where Kenneth could find it easily, and waited.

The lieutenant entered the tent once again, this time with a mug of coffee in his hand. He sipped it and grimaced, then walked right past the portrait. Eros frowned and quickly placed it where the man would probably turn next. But Hathaway turned the other way and missed it entirely, gazing at the mirror and rubbing the morning stubble upon his chin instead. He sat down on a camp stool and began to look through one of his kit bags.

"I need a shave . . . Jackson! Where's my razor?" he yelled toward the entrance of the tent. He took another mouthful of coffee.

"Idiot," muttered Eros, feeling frustrated, and dropped the miniature in Kenneth's lap.

The lieutenant choked and jumped up from his seat, spilling coffee over his hand and coughing. He held the dripping mug away from him and stared at the portrait that had fallen to the ground. He took in a deep breath and rubbed his hand over his face.

"Damn," Kenneth whispered, turning a little pale. He tenderly picked up the miniature and wiped it on his shirt and sighed. "I'll be seeing snakes in my soup next. No more bottles of French brandy for you, my boy." He drained his mug in a quick gulp. "I need more coffee."

Eros stood next to him, poised with an arrow in his hand. It would take one little scratch, just at the right time. . . .

Hathaway turned toward the tent entrance again. "And, Jackson, bring me more coffee while you're at it," he roared. He turned back to the miniature and smiled tenderly at it. "My dear, sweet, gentle Aimee," he murmured.

Eros struck. He jabbed the point of the arrow into Kenneth's arm like a spear.

Hathaway absently slapped at the apparent sting, as if at an annoying gnat. His face softened as he gazed at the portrait. "Wonderful Aimee," he sighed. "Glorious, beautiful, perfect Aimee." His expression became fervent and his eyes seemed to glow. "The best of all women, the epitome of womanhood, a *goddess* among women." He closed his eyes and reverently kissed the miniature. "It's a damn bloody *sign* from heaven the way it fell into my lap. She's somehow watching over me, praying for me, I know it." He looked around the tent, and seeing a sturdy bit of string, strung it through a tiny loop at the top of the portrait frame, then hung it around his neck. "Her prayers must be what saved me all those times. An angel, that's what she is."

Eros frowned, feeling a little put out. He knew Miss

Mattingly's devotion to her betrothed was strong, but it was his own intervention that had protected the man. He'd expended a great deal of energy trying to keep Hathaway out of trouble, and warfare was not his forte. He shrugged. Well, it did not matter. Psyche's brother was well taken care of now; he'd done what she asked of him.

A sharp cry sounded from the tent in which Hathaway had deposited the woman, making Eros quickly leave Hathaway's side. He grinned. Well, wartime or not, there were sometimes opportunities for love. He got out an arrow and his bow and shot an arrow into Pargeter's tent.

"You, Ensign! Boy! What the devil are you doing?" came Hathaway's voice behind him.

Startled, Eros turned, almost dropping his second arrow. Kenneth had come out of his tent and was looking straight at him with a puzzled look in his eyes, as if trying to place him. Was his invisibility wearing away? Quickly he brought all his god-energies to bear upon himself, and saw the lieutenant pale and close his eyes briefly. "I need more coffee," he heard him say, and watched him go back into his tent.

This was not good, Eros thought. It was best if he left Spain and returned to England as soon as possible. The lieutenant would do just as well by himself; the troops were to rest, then march for a while, so he would be in relative safety. If he were to watch over Hathaway while he was on campaign, he needed to leave from time to time so as to preside over his own specialty and gain back the energy he had lost.

Doubt niggled at the back of Eros's mind as he left the camp. There had been more than a bit of worshipfulness in Hathaway's voice and manner toward Aimee's portrait . . . but that was all to the good, he was certain. What woman did not like to be worshiped, after all?

He shrugged. All would be well, and the next time a chance at furlough came up, Lieutenant Hathaway would be sure to go home and devote himself to his betrothed in a very satisfying way.

# Chapter 1

London, 1814

The smell of soot and crowded people pressed upon Captain Kenneth Hathaway as he walked from his lodgings to his family's home. He was not used to the smells, or to the cries of the baker's boys and shouts of crow-voiced tradesmen hawking their wares all around him. The sounds beat upon him like an alien drum, making him walk faster toward home, hoping to find something familiar again.

He'd been in other towns and cities with the similar noises and scents, but his stay in them had always been of short duration. Battlefields had been his home, until the smell of gunpowder, horses, blood, and dry dust had seemed more a part of his life than this city, so crowded and confusing.

He shook his head. In his dreams, England had been full of green fields and sweet grass. Even the sky did not conform to his imaginings, for clouds obscured the sun, and whatever blue did show was sooty and dull.

But this was London, and of course what he had dreamed of was his home near Tunbridge Wells. He smiled wryly at himself. He was going to see Aimee, his betrothed, and however disappointing London was, he knew she would meet his every expectation.

Slowing his steps, he took out the miniature of her from inside his coat, and he let out a long sigh. He'd gazed at this portrait so many times, he knew each stroke of paint upon it like he knew his own heart. But he never tired of looking at it; how could anyone not wish to look at a goddess?

He whistled a little tune as he walked up the steps of his father's house. He would put the war, everything, all behind him, and look forward to seeing Aimee again. It had been too long since he'd seen her.

It was spring, it was unusually warm, and the pale blue sky that peeked between the filmy clouds would have beckoned anyone to leave the indoors to drive to the park, or walk with a friend to some shops. But Miss Aimee Mattingly sat inside the Hathaways' London town house, clasping and unclasping her hands in her lap, and tried not to look at the clock. Kenneth had sent a note home saying he would come to call at two o'clock, and now it was half-past two. What could be keeping him?

She pulled her lower lip between her teeth, then released it. Gnawing on her lip would do nothing to speed him. Taking a deep breath, she made herself relax, and even smiled at herself. She had waited for her betrothed for three years—and now she felt impatient because he was late by thirty minutes? Ridiculous!

Rearranging her dress around her for the tenth time, Aimee made herself sit back on her chair, and folded her hands in her lap. Would Kenneth look different? It was only three years, after all, could anyone change much in that time? On the other hand, with all the battles and deprivation he'd experienced in Wellington's army, it would not be surprising if he had changed.

She had met him five years ago at her uncle's estate when she was only fifteen and Kenneth was nineteen. He had slipped away from Cambridge during holiday with her cousin Bertram Garthwaite and had come to her uncle's house. It had been only a week since she had come to live there; both her parents had died of the bloody flux, and her kindly uncle, Squire Garthwaite, had been named her guardian in her father's will.

There had been, apparently, a prizefight in the area that Bertram and Kenneth had wanted to attend, and since the squire was very knowledgeable about such matters, he was able to inform them of the whereabouts and invited Kenneth to stay with them. Kenneth had been a handsome youth, and when her cousin had introduced them, he had smiled in an admiring yet mischievous way at her. Her attraction to him had been instantaneous, and she had spent part of the day thinking of him.

But the other part of the day had been spent in weeping for her parents, for she missed them dreadfully, and it was when Kenneth had found her alone in the conservatory that her attraction had turned to love. For despite the delay it would cause in getting to the prizefight, he had sat down next to her and held her hand, listening to her speak of her parents. When she had finished, he had taken his handkerchief—for hers had become quite sodden by then—and dabbed the last of the tears from her cheeks, and then kissed where he had just dabbed, and then, gently, her lips.

She had fallen in love with him and in the weeks and months afterward he had come to visit, her love grew stronger. She loved the way he looked, his kindness, his daring ways and teasing manner. She also loved the kisses he snatched in private, the way he had touched her and held her close to him. It seemed he had loved her, too, for he tried to see her whenever possible, and when he quit Cambridge to join the army, he begged her to marry him. She had agreed, although both of them knew her uncle would say she was too young. And so he did; but at least he agreed to their betrothal, and they had to be content with that.

In truth, she was grateful, even so. Kenneth could have looked higher for a prospective wife, for he would be a baronet some day, and had a sizable fortune of his own. And though she had a good dowry herself, her birth good, and Kenneth's family content with his choice, there was no denying that if it had not been for his mother's generous invitation to stay at the Hathaway town house and offer to sponsor her in society, she would never have seen the inside of Almack's hallowed halls.

Aimee sighed and glanced at the clock again. But now the fighting had ceased, for Bonaparte was exiled at Elba; Kenneth would come home at last, and soon they would be married.

A heavy tread sounded outside the door, and Aimee looked up. The door swung open and Kenneth Hathaway strode forward into the parlor. Her hand flew up nervously to the high neck of her dress and she stood up. "Kenneth?"

"Aimee?" He stopped in front of her and frowned, staring at her intently from head to foot.

Aimee clutched her skirts, feeling at once nervous and downcast. This was not what she had envisioned his return to be. But it had been quite a long time, and she had new clothes now . . . no doubt she was not what he had expected. And certainly he had changed, though she would know him anywhere. She put on a smile, holding out her hands to him.

"Kenneth . . . I am glad you are home."

He started, as if he had been thinking of something else, and smiled at last. He came to her and took her hand and brought it to his lips, gently, tenderly, as if he held something delicate and rare. He lifted his head and smiled, "Beautiful Aimee! How I have missed you."

"Oh!" gasped Aimee, blushing, as he sat in a chair nearby. She smiled shyly. "I have missed you, too. You—you have changed a little."

Kenneth gave a wide grin. His strong, arched nose was the same, as was his square and stubborn chin. But his smile was white in his now tanned face, his light blue eyes looked penetratingly pale in contrast, and his dark auburn hair now had blond streaks in it. Aimee remembered him as tall when he had left, but he seemed even taller than that now. He'd been one-and-twenty years of age back then, and slighter of form. But now his shoulders amply filled out his scarlet regimentals, though his face was leaner than she remembered it. And his long, lanky legs were no longer lanky but well-muscled—She brought her eyes hastily up to his face again.

If possible, Kenneth's grin was wider than ever. "I daresay I have changed more than a little. I'm a captain now, did I tell you? Do you remember when I wrote you about the march to Salamanca? I didn't think a man could grow any more past the age of twenty. Well I did, and I had a devil of a time finding a well-fitting pair of b—" He stopped.

Aimee's alarmed eyes flew to his.

"Boots." He laughed. "You have not altered in the least, little Miss Priss! You always did rise so easily to bait!"

She chuckled. "And you have always been a terrible tease, Kenneth! *That* has not changed in you at all!"

But he had changed, more than she'd seen when he first walked in the room. He had been a restless youth when she had first met him, and that liveliness had turned into an intense masculine vitality, which seemed almost too much for the dainty chair in which he sat. She glanced at him, and wondered if the chair could contain him, for he moved constantly, his booted foot tapping the floor while his eyes almost hungrily scanned the well-appointed room, the windows, and the tasteful furniture. He ran his hand back through his hair, but it did little good: a stray lock fell forward onto his forehead. His eyes returned to Aimee, and he looked her over keenly.

"You have changed, too, Aimee. Have you done something with your hair? I thought it was lighter than that."

Aimee self-consciously put her hand to her head. "No, I have merely styled it differently, and I certainly would not have dyed it!"

A slightly alarmed look came into Kenneth's eyes. "Devil take it—er, that is, deuce take it, I didn't mean to imply that you had! Dam—er, dash it all, I'm sorry, Aimee. Thing is, I've been away for so long, and the only thing I've had to look at is your miniature." He took the little portrait out from his jacket pocket and gazed at it, smiling tenderly. He looked at her again, assessingly, and a slight frowning crease formed between his brows. "I suppose you haven't changed all that much. You don't know what a relief that is. Your letter mentioned your uncle had let you come to London for your come-out—I thought you'd have turned into a sophisticated miss."

"I? Sophisticated? Oh, no! You know I blush too easily for that."

"Yes, I know." Kenneth reached out and briefly touched her cheek. His hand felt rough and callused, and she wondered what sort of work he must have done to make it so. "My sweet English rose—all blond and white and blushing pink. Do you know I dreamed of all this— of you, of being here?"

"Did—did you?" Aimee breathed. A swell of love overflowed her heart. She had been so right to have agreed to marry him, despite her uncle's protest that she had been too young to know her own mind at the time.

"Yes. Fresh and untouched. Everything war is not." His eyes seemed to darken, as if a shadow had passed across his face. Then he grinned at her in his old way.

How fanciful she was being! As if he could be anything but happy when he was safely returned to England! She looked shyly up at him. "I . . . I have missed you very much, Kenneth. I suppose I shall see you for dinner?"

"Ah, no, I am afraid I cannot. I have yet to see to a few details at headquarters."

"But you must have dinner at some time! And Psyche looks different from when you last saw her—she has grown up, you know, and is making her come-out with me this season. Cassandra may even come to dine today, since her husband has been called away on some estate matter. But then perhaps you've already seen her."

"Er, no, not yet." An embarrassed look came over his face.

"But, Kenneth, it has been all of two days since you have arrived in London!"

"Well, I was not altogether sure of my reception. . . ."

"Oh, heavens! It has been ages since you argued with your father and went off to the army instead of staying at Cambridge as he wanted you to do. He would not hold a grudge against you that long!"

"No, but he will pinch at me about it! You know how I hate that! Besides, I have been busy settling matters with my regiment before I went on furlough. I have responsibilities, you know." He still looked uncomfortable, however. "I did write them a note saying I was coming home." He smiled tenderly at her and rose from his chair, then knelt on one knee in front of her. "Come, my heart, don't be angry at me." He took her hand and kissed it reverently. "I worship you, you know I do. I will do anything you say, I swear it."

Aimee laughed. "How terrible you are! As if you ever worshiped me. I think teasing so that you will escape a scold is more like it!"

Kenneth frowned slightly and shook his head. He pulled something out from the pocket of his coat and held it up. It was the portrait she had given him before he left for the army. "But of course I mean it." He gazed at the miniature and a fervent light grew in his eyes. "I adore you—haven't I said it? You are the most perfect woman in England, an angel whose prayers have kept me safe through all the battles I've been in. I would have died if it hadn't been for the thought of you waiting for me at home."

Aimee gazed at him, and a tendril of unease crept through her joy in seeing Kenneth again. She was used to his teasing, his restlessness, and loved the tender looks he gave her. But he had a different air about him now, and when he said he worshiped her it seemed he was not teasing at all. There was indeed an ardent, even reverent, light in his eyes when he looked at her portrait and then at herself. It was not something she was used to, from him or anyone else. She was just Miss Aimee Mattingly, quite ordinary—well-born, it was true, but no more than that. She had never thought she would be someone to idolize.

However, it was certainly very flattering. There were not many young ladies who could claim such devotion from her betrothed. He must love her very much indeed. She smiled tenderly at him.

"I think I cannot claim such a thing, Kenneth, but I do know I love you."

The worshipfulness in his eyes grew and he held her hand tightly, kissing it over and over again. "God, how I adore you. You don't know how it was over there—the blood, the death—no, I won't sully your ears with it. But I thought of you, and it was for you I did it, for you I proved myself. I would die a thousand deaths for you, you know."

The unease she felt before unfurled into definite discomfort. She gave a hesitant laugh. "I hope you do not! I would prefer you very much alive, Kenneth."

He kissed her hand again. "You are a queen, a god—"

The door opened suddenly and a petite red-haired young lady stepped into the parlor. "Aimee, I must tell you—the drollest thing! I saw—" She stopped suddenly and stared at the man before her.

"Kenneth . . . ?" she whispered, her hand rising to her trembling lips.

He rose and grinned at her. "Yes, it's me, Psyche."

"Oh, Kenneth!" his sister shrieked. She ran to him and hugged him fiercely. He gave her a smacking kiss on her cheek and she pushed away from him. "We didn't know—when did you—" She stopped, and anger flared suddenly in her eyes. "Oh, you odious—! Why did you not tell us when you were coming home?" She thumped her fist against his chest. "You only sent that stupid note saying you were returning and nothing else, not whether you were well or ill or anything! How *could* you?"

Kenneth shrugged irritably. "I didn't have much time. We were about to leave—"

"Surely you had time enough to write more than 'will be home soon, yours, Kenneth'? Why, Mama has been mad with worry over you—she has saved enough lint and bandages to wrap around all of Wellington's army. Papa has been so distracted that he forgets his spectacles at least three times a day instead of only once. And we daren't tell Cassandra, for she is increasing—"

"What, again?" Kenneth asked.

"She and Paul are *very* much in love, so I expect that would have something to do with it," Psyche said primly.

"I imagine so," Kenneth said, grinning widely.

His sister looked at him suspiciously, but continued. "Anyway, Cassandra would worry also, and that would not be good for her. But I would think that you should have at least told Aimee you were well and had arrived."

"Well, I did."

Psyche looked inquiringly at Aimee, a hurt look in her eyes.

"Only an hour ago!" Aimee protested.

"An hour!" Psyche turned accusingly to her brother.

He gave her an impatient look, not deigning to answer.

"I know what it is," Psyche said. "You are afraid of one of Papa's lectures."

"Nonsense! I doubt he'll lecture me—he hasn't sent one of those sorts of letters to me for a year at least."

"Kenneth, I think you do mind it," Aimee said gently. "You said as much only a while ago."

He turned to her, remorse in his eyes. "Ah, dev—deuce take it! Very well!" He went to Aimee and held her hand tightly in his, gazing at her with clear devotion. "I can't bear it when you look at me like that. It's true, you know how I hate getting a bear-garden jaw from Father."

Aimee pressed his hand to her cheek. "Perhaps he won't do it this time. I am sure he misses you quite terribly."

He smiled at her. "You're an angel, Aimee."

Aimee blushed and shook her head. "Oh, no!" She could not help feeling pleased, even though she was not used to such praise. She saw Psyche give her brother a quick, puzzled look, and unease rose in her again. Did Psyche also think that he was not acting quite himself? It occurred to Aimee that she had never heard such words from him before. He had called her "sweet" and "love"—

the small endearments of a lover. Aside from that, his speech had always been straightforward and blunt. He was not even above the language of the stables, when he forgot himself. But she could not recall him being so . . . effusive before. Perhaps the war had changed him, although she would have thought it would have made him more coarse in his speech than effusive.

"Perhaps you should stay—I am afraid I have promised to see my great-aunt at dinner. But we shall have plenty of time together later," Aimee said. She did not know what made her say this, for she had thought she'd want to spend all her time with him when he came back from the continent—but promises were promises and she had made one to her great-aunt May. This time she saw Psyche give her a quizzical look. She smiled at her friend and then at her betrothed. "I do not want to be selfish you see—how could I let Lady Hathaway build up more than an army's worth of worry for you, Kenneth?"

He seized her hand once more and covered it with kisses. "You are a *goddess* among women!" he said fervently.

She pulled her hand away sharply. "No, Kenneth, I am only Aimee, your betrothed." He looked at her, startled, and then smiled at her.

"The best of women, then," he said. "And the most modest."

She saw Psyche stare at her brother, frown, then shake her head slightly. "I think Aimee is right, Kenneth. You will get more of a scold if you don't come home."

He gave his sister a wry smile. "Oh, very well! I suppose I should . . . but don't expect me to squire you to any musicales now that I'm in town. You know how tedious I find them."

Aimee sighed in relief. *That* sounded more like her Kenneth. He was not very musical, despite Cassandra and Psyche's definite talent for it, and despite his own pleasant tenor singing voice.

Kenneth left then, pressing another kiss on Aimee's hand before he left, and Psyche went upstairs to change her clothes. Aimee went to the window to watch her betrothed walk down the street. She sighed and touched the hand that Kenneth had kissed so fervently . . . and found she was creasing her dress quite badly. She relaxed her hand and smoothed out her dress.

His homecoming was not quite what she had expected . . . in truth, it was more than she expected. Her betrothed had left, a restless, impulsive, teasing youth, and now he had come back, a stranger. She shook her head at herself and smiled. How stupid she was! Any other lady would have been overjoyed at the man he'd become—handsome, obviously loyal, adoring, and romantic. What woman would not want a man to call her an angel, a goddess? He had knelt at her feet, and if he had not kissed the hem of her gown, certainly he had kissed her hand with all the reverence a woman could hope for. To have a betrothed as Kenneth was now was every woman's dream.

The image of Psyche's joy at seeing her brother came to her again, and she remembered how fiercely she had hugged him. And then she remembered that he had touched her cheek only briefly with his hand, and when he kissed her, it was only on her hand.

He had not touched her in any other way. Aimee closed her eyes and remembered, years ago, how he had kissed her mouth, long and deep; how he had held her in his arms, pressing her close to him as if he could not bear to part from her. He had done none of that this time, though they had been private together in the parlor long enough for them to have been able to do so. She had been glad that both of their families acknowledged the betrothal, for she did not need a chaperone any longer when they were together. But he had not taken advantage of it, as he had before.

Did he not remember the way it had been between them? It had been three years—it was a long time, and he had been through terrible battles, and had even suffered grievous wounds once, or so his letters had said. She had worried so, then, afraid he would not recover from the fever he had contracted. Was that what had changed him? She did not know.

One could not change the past, of course. She had learned that when her parents had died, and quite thoroughly. Perhaps he had forgotten their kisses, and she could forgive that, for war, illness, and death were terrible ordeals. She had not experienced war, to be sure, but she knew about illness and death, and how one's life and perceptions could change because of it. Perhaps this had happened to Kenneth, also, and the violence that had surrounded him could not have made it any better.

She sighed, then made herself smile. Kenneth was home now, and they could start over, perhaps. They could discover kisses together once again, and that would be quite wonderful, she was sure.

# Chapter 2

Kenneth walked slowly back to his lodgings. Nothing had come up to his expectations, not London, not England, not even Aimee. But he had been expecting something . . . more. He remembered, years ago, when he had first courted Aimee. He had marveled at the way the sun caught her hair and made it shine in ripples of gold, and how her lips would part in eagerness and made him want to kiss her again and again. He was, actually, surprised at the way Aimee looked. He remembered her being beautiful, pale, serene, and majestic, a slender goddess of a woman—taller, in fact.

To tell the truth, he'd received a bit of a shock, seeing her. Oh, she was a pretty enough girl, to be sure. But she wasn't tall, not by any means. She came up to his chin, and slender—well, she was very small at the waist, from what he could tell when her dress draped against it. But the rest of her was full of curves. Even her mouth was full and curled at the corners, not the perfect slender bow he had thought she'd had. Her hair was blond, it was true, but it was not the pale gold in the miniature he carried, but the color of bright daffodils. And her nose had not the perfect straight Grecian lines he'd expected but just a bit of a tilt at the end.

What was worse was that he hadn't wanted to kiss her as he used to when he was courting her. He remembered wanting to kiss her all the time, wanting to kiss her everywhere he could—or thought he did. He rubbed his hand over his eyes. God, he didn't know what he wanted! One moment he wanted to worship at her feet, and the next he wished he were out of the engagement out of sheer disappointment. That was the word with no bark on it. He was disappointed and tired and wanted the bloody hell out of London. It was boring, too, now that the battles were over, and the diplomats doing their work. He wasn't a man for dancing and didn't care to go to balls and such, and he knew his mother would expect him to escort her and Psyche to them. Well, he'd do his duty as he always did, but only just.

Kenneth entered the hotel—Grillon's—in which he lodged and went up the stairs to his rooms. It was a well-appointed apartment and had everything he could wish, but he grimaced at the clothes piled upon the chair in his bedroom. He would need to get a valet soon; he was running out of his store of clothes, and though he had plenty of funds with which to buy more, he hated the process of procuring and buying a new suit. He shrugged out of his uniform and draped it carefully across the back of the chair on which he had piled the clothes. Somehow this was not what he had envisioned either, being away from his family when he returned. Perhaps he should have just lodged in his family's town house—there would have been enough room, he was sure. But the thought of having so many people around about him—he shuddered. He wanted to be alone, at least for a while, until he became used to being home again.

He sighed. Perhaps his time away at war had painted his memories a brighter color. If he had thought of gold, it had been in coin he didn't have, and if he thought of kisses it had been something so far away as to be a dream. Perhaps that was it—he had dreamed so much of what he did not have that he had built castles in the air, brighter than anything made of homely stone, and now reality had blasted a hole in the ramparts.

For what, then, had he fought? He walked restlessly to the window of his room and looked out of it. The sky had turned more gray than before. He turned away, walking to the mantelpiece to fiddle with some ornaments there, then back to the window again, pacing. There had been so many times in battle when he had wished to turn and flee, or drop his sword and lie down amongst the dead from weariness. Just thinking of it even now brought a deep-down fatigue pulling at the very bones of his body. He had thought he'd fought for his country, but when he saw his countrymen dead around him on foreign soil, it seemed to make little sense. He'd fought for loyalty to his commander, and then for Aimee—or what he had built up of Aimee. Had he fought, then, only for illusions?

*You are not at war now. It is over.* Illusions or not, he was in England now, not Spain, and he'd better get used to it. He shook his head at himself. He would have thought he'd wade into English life—soothing and refreshing after the heat and work of battle. But he could not rid himself of an edginess, an odd anxiety that he needed to be ready—for what? No battle would happen here. And in truth, all he needed—all he truly wanted— was to marry Aimee and live comfortably with her as her husband.

Husband. Another odd thing, and he could not help thinking it. He wondered suddenly if he were truly ready for it. Of course he wished to marry Aimee. Who would not want to marry a goddess?

His steps slowed, then stopped, and he gazed out the window again. A goddess was not something one married. Worshiped, yes. Adored, yes. But somehow the idea of bedding a goddess left him cold. He took out the portrait of Aimee from his pocket and gazed at it. Again the feeling of adoration rose in him, and he forced the feeling down this time. What did he truly feel? He imagined himself lying with the coolly beautiful woman in the portrait, imagined her response to his kisses . . . and all he could think of was the response of a marble statue—cold, unfeeling. And he was committed to a lifetime of feeling this way.

Bloody hell. He was betrothed to her. He couldn't break off the engagement, of course. Of course he'd marry her because he was honor-bound to do it. He thought of other men who had married cold women and how they'd found a warm and comfortable mistress, and something in him rebelled at it. Perhaps it was the residue of his dreams when he'd been in Spain—Aimee warm and loving, the way she'd curl up comfortably in his arms in the months during his courtship. Or at least, that was what he had thought he'd remembered. But the only thing he could think of when he looked at the portrait was how he adored her, how he wanted to kiss her feet and worship the ground she walked upon—but not, really, how he wanted to touch her.

Kenneth closed his hand over the portrait and quickly walked to the desk in his chamber and opened a drawer. He put the portrait facedown in it and then closed the drawer—or tried to. At first he thought the drawer was stuck, but then realized to his surprise that he had not let go of the portrait. He swallowed. He didn't want to put it away, was the truth of it. It was as if he'd gazed on Aimee's picture so long and had put so much of his hope into it during the long hard course of war that he could not let it go now.

It isn't real. It is just a portrait. But his hand clutched it tighter so that the frame's metal rim cut into his hand. Slowly he took it out of the desk drawer again and almost, almost gazed at it again. But he slipped it into the pocket of his jacket instead. An odd, uneasy feeling settled into the pit of his stomach as he pressed his hands down upon the surface of the desk. If he did not know better, he'd almost think the portrait had somehow ensorcelled him, that somehow he'd fallen in love with it instead of Aimee. Nonsense, of course.

He pressed a hand upon his forehead for a moment, then shook his head. He didn't want to admit to it, but he'd seen it before: battle fatigue. It made a man act in ways that made no sense, and it was no respecter of rank. He despised himself for it—it was a weakness, and one that a man never admitted to, at least in public. But he'd seen it in the dazed eyes of officers and enlisted men alike. It made them restless and sleepless even though they were tired down to their very bones, and drink more than was good for them. It was why so many of them became inebriated after battle—to let them sleep. But no one ever admitted it—bad for the men's morale if you were an officer.

And his men had had it bad enough with all the deprivations they had had to go through without letting them know the number of times he'd wanted to quit after the first rush of battle. A sudden wish to confess it all to someone overwhelmed him . . . but of course he could not. He was not sure if he could bear the skeptical or pitying looks he was sure he'd get, and what if there were to be another war soon? France and the other countries Bonaparte had taken over were still uneasy with each other. Lord only knew if that uneasiness would break out in more disputes and battle again. And he was sure anyone he told would remember . . . No, he could not tell anyone.

Well, he was a soldier, was he not? And it was a soldier's lot to bear what he must, wherever he must be. He almost took out Aimee's portrait again, but stopped himself, only patting the pocket above his heart. Certainly marriage—however disillusioning—was better than war, and much easier to bear.

But there was one part of him that wished he did not have to bear one more thing, that he could exorcise the ever-present restlessness and sink himself into deep and unceasing sleep.

Psyche absently selected a necklace from her box and handed it to her maid to fasten behind her neck. There was something . . . wrong about Kenneth. He had changed somehow. She supposed anyone must if they went through the horrors of war. It was a terrible experience, if his letters came anything close to the truth, and she was sure he had not mentioned everything he had seen. But there was something else that had changed in him.

She gazed in the mirror and made a face at herself. She looked well enough, she supposed, but her face looked too pale and there was nothing to be done about her unfashionably red hair. It curled every which way, and would not stay where it was combed. However, her maid had come up with a particularly good way of dealing with it—she had brought it up to a knot at the top of her head and let the curls cascade down around her face to her shoulders. It was a negligent, casual style, but it served its purpose: it did not matter if it went every which way, because it looked as if it was supposed to.

She chuckled. It was odd to compare her brother to a style of dressing hair, but Kenneth was that way, too. He was always one to go every which way, but you knew it was his nature and he could not help it. The army had been perfect for him. It gave him the discipline he needed, but he could be as wild as his nature allowed when in the midst of battle. Even her father, Sir John Hathaway, had acknowledged it had done Kenneth some good, though he still did not like it. He did not want to lose his only son and heir, after all.

She dismissed her maid and then took a red ribbon from a drawer. Well, she could not do anything about her hair, but she could do something about her cheeks. Her mother frowned on paint, but it wasn't as if she were actually using paint on her face, after all, only wetting the ribbon a little and dabbing it on her cheeks. She dipped one end of the ribbon in the washbowl and pressed it to one cheek and then the other, smoothing the color until it blended with her skin. There!

"I think you look better without it, actually."

Psyche started and almost upset the washbowl. "Harry! I wish you would not come up behind me like that!" She gazed in the mirror at the tall, golden-haired youth behind her and frowned. How unjust it was that his hair—though it curled just as much as hers—always seemed to be perfectly in order. On the other hand, it was much shorter than hers; perhaps that was the answer.

Her friend looked at her critically. "I think the color is wrong for you. You should use a warmer color if you are going to paint your face."

"I am *not* painting my face—not precisely. I am only making myself look . . . not so pale."

Harry leaned against a bedpost and grinned, his wings waving lazily. "You should be grateful. I understand an interesting pallor is all the rage."

"Only if one is considered a sylph, and I doubt I will ever be considered one—why, only look at me!" She spread out her arms.

Harry's gaze went from her head to her feet and slowly back up again. His grin grew wider. "No, not a sylph, for you are too plump in the bosom for that. Sylphs tend to be seriously lacking that way. See, you are blushing quite nicely, so you do not need the ribbon at all."

"How odious you are! You should not talk to me in such a way," Psyche said, frowning. "I do not know if I should be complimented or insulted."

"Oh, complimented, of course. I have very good taste, you know."

"Hmph!"

"It's true! Do you remember Mary Flannery last Season?"

"Yeeesss . . ."

"Hardly noticeable—mouse-colored hair, flat-chested, and shy. One of your sylphs." Harry took out an arrow from his quiver and twirled it between his fingers in a contemplative sort of way. "But she did have a certain piquant—though hidden—*je ne sais quoi*. I saw it immediately. It took only a few suggestions in her ear and she was proclaimed a diamond of the first water."

Psyche paused in putting on her earrings and gazed at him, surprised. "You actually spoke to her? She saw you?"

"No, of course not, although I have been thinking lately it would be amusing to be seen every once in a while." He shrugged. "But it was a simple thing to whisper a few suggestions just as she was falling asleep so that she changed her style completely. And married an earl, too."

Psyche beamed at him. "How very kind of you to put her in the way of things! I remember she was dreadfully shy and quite plain-looking when she first came out. But she improved immensely, and see how happy she is now!" She went to him and squeezed his hand, holding it to her cheek briefly.

He glanced at her, then pulled his hand away, and she was surprised to see his ears turn pink. She grinned. She had never seen him blush before in all the years she had known him from the time she'd been a child, and she had a terrible urge to make him blush again, for he could be horridly toplofty. Certainly she would think about it, and see if she could do it later.

She returned to her earrings, peering into the mirror to see that she had them positioned correctly. "Well," she said. "I wish you would whisper a few words into Kenneth's ear. He has come home at last, you know. I saw him today—he did not want to face Papa first! But he acted so strangely! Not toward me, of course—he was his usual teasing self. But he was not so to Aimee, and he always had been before."

There was a brief silence before Harry said, "Oh?" Psyche looked at him suspiciously, but his expression was unconcerned.

"Yes," she continued. "But this time—he seemed almost about to salaam at her feet like an Indian native! Although I must admit it might be something that most ladies might like, poor Aimee looked quite uncomfortable."

"She will become used to it, I am sure," Harry said.

There seemed to be an odd note in his voice, and Psyche stared at him for a moment. "Have you done anything to Kenneth?"

"I?" Harry's face was bland, but she noted how his wings fluttered in an uncomfortable manner.

"Yes, you! Who else would have something to do in such a matter?"

Harry shrugged. "You asked me to watch over him while he was at war, and so I did. It is much too easy for a man to become unfaithful when under such trials and when away from his beloved. So . . . I made sure your brother would not. That has a great deal to do with his welfare, I believe, and you *did* ask me to take care of him."

"Oh, heavens." Psyche stared at her friend, and dread curled up in the pit of her stomach. She remembered the troubles he had got her sister and her husband into the last time he had let loose his arrows, and she did not look forward to more. "How many?" she demanded.

Harry let out an impatient sigh. "Only one! I had heard too many jokes about how your brother 'hath a way' with the ladies, and wished to make sure such jokes did not become truth. So I shot him while he was looking at a portrait of Aimee."

Psyche gnawed her lower lip as she gazed at Harry. Perhaps it was not such a bad thing—she well knew how wild Kenneth had been at Cambridge, and his friend Bertie Garthwaite had even let it slip that Kenneth had associated with ladies who were less than virtuous in their behavior. If Harry's shooting Kenneth had kept him faithful to Aimee, surely that could not hurt. She nodded briskly.

"Well, I suppose that's all right, then. But no more shooting arrows at Kenneth, if you please!"

"Of course," Harry said carelessly.

"Hmph!" Psyche said, then went downstairs to dinner.

"It wasn't far from the stream to the camp," Kenneth said, chuckling. "But the damn—er, dashed cliffs were steep and the only way back was over a rocky path. Nobody liked to fetch the water, but with half the enlisted men gone or on other duty, Pargeter was forced to get it himself. It'd rained the day before so of course he got his boots muddied and was cursing his head off the whole way back. But it was just as well he was preoccupied. What he didn't know was that he'd picked up a tarantula on one tassel of his boots—you should have seen him dance when I pointed it out! And he dropped the bucket and had to go down and refill it again."

Psyche laughed, but there was a decided silence from one end of the table (interrupted by a single "hmph!" at the mention of their cousin Pargeter) and continued muffled sniffling at the other.

"Oh, poor boy!" cried Lady Hathaway. "How horrible for you! I am so glad you did not get stung by such a creature. But you must not talk further—you are so thin! Here—do take another slice of roast beef, and there are still some green peas, too."

"No, really, Mother, I have eaten quite enough." He patted his stomach and smiled.

Lady Hathaway gazed at him anxiously. "Is the food too rich for you perhaps? Would you like some soup?"

"No! Er, that is, no, thank you."

Psyche laughed again. "How can you say that, Mama, when he has filled his plate twice and eaten it all? He can hardly fatten himself up all at once, you know."

Lady Hathaway smiled wryly at Psyche and then her son. "I am sorry, Kenneth. It is just that you have changed so, and I am not used to seeing you so lean."

Kenneth grinned at her. "Oh, I'll fatten up soon enough if I take my dinners at home. But I mustn't do that, you know. I'll be unfit and certainly too heavy for my horse if I do." But he shifted uncomfortably on his chair. Thank God Psyche was at dinner; he did not seem to be able to get much of a conversation from his mother other than about his health and her anxious queries about any possible injuries. His father, on the other hand, said very little and only gazed at him in that remote, slightly interested way that always unnerved him.

"Going back to your quarters, are you?" Sir John asked abruptly, his eyebrows raised.

Kenneth gazed at him, wondering if there was anything behind his father's words. He felt he was a disappointment to him, for though he could have passed the exams at Cambridge, he had had no patience for his studies and had left as soon as he could save up enough money to buy a commission in the army. Further, his father had wanted him to go to Oxford instead, but his rebellious nature at the time insisted on Cambridge. But he knew his father was a man of tremendous intellect and Kenneth felt he was always undergoing some scholarly examination whenever his father talked to him.

"Yes," Kenneth replied, suppressing an urge to fidget.

"Ah." Silence, then: "I thought perhaps you would resign your commission now that Bonaparte has gone to Elba."

"I was thinking of it," Kenneth said. "But one never knows when one's country may have need of my services." There, that should put paid to his father's questions.

"I had hoped you might come home and attend to the estate."

Kenneth rolled his eyes. "Dash it all, you know I have no talent for estate matters. Best leave it to the bailiff."

Sir John looked at him sternly. "You may not have a talent for it, but it is your responsibility. As honest as Grisham is, a man's land is best overseen by the owner, not the hired hands."

"Best! Why you know what a muddle I made of the accounts the last time!"

"It is only because you refused to apply yourself!"

"Apply myself! Why, I spent an hour over those account books!"

"An hour is hardly going to acquaint you with the matters to which you must attend!"

"John! Kenneth!" cried Lady Hathaway, shaking her finger at them. "Here is our family at last together, and what must both of you do but argue as soon as we are at dinner! Is this the sort of respect that the army has taught you, Kenneth?"

Kenneth pressed his lips together. "No, Mother. It is not. I am sorry, Father."

"And you, John! Our son is newly come home, and you cannot stop from airing old grievances!"

Sir John gazed at her for a long moment, then turned to Kenneth. "It . . . has been difficult without you, son."

Kenneth nodded, about to reply, then noted Psyche gazing wide-eyed at both of them. He smiled at her. "And just to prove that I can contribute to the family in some way, I promise to escort my dear sister to a ball." He noticed, from the corner of his eye, that his father sighed and attended to his plate again. For one moment, he felt he should say something to his father, but a little laugh from Psyche caught his attention.

She looked at him consideringly, a gleam in her eyes. "I think you should escort me to some balls, an assembly or two, and to Almack's." She grinned when he made a face at her.

"Oh, very well! But you must promise to dance with Bertie Garthwaite if I do. He has a *tendre* for you, you know."

Psyche laughed. "What a tease you are! All Bertie can talk of is food, so I hardly think he is interested in me."

"I think it's your hair. It probably reminds him of a goulash of carrots."

"How horrid you are! I am half inclined not to go with you to any ball at all—"

Kenneth interrupted with an exaggerated sigh of relief. "Good. That means I won't have to go to Almack's."

"—but of course we shall and I will be sure to introduce you to the worst dancer at each function." Psyche grinned mischievously at him. "There is Lady Connington's ball coming up in two weeks, so I am sure you may be ready for it by then."

"Two weeks! That is hardly enough time for me to find a decent coat for a ball. I shall have to wear something quite shabby."

"You know you may wear your regimentals, so you cannot get out of it that way," Psyche said.

Kenneth gave a large sigh. "How I suffer for what I do for my sister."

"Nonsense! You may not like it when first you go, but you always end up flirting with every lady there, so I am sure you cannot find it all that tedious."

"You forget, I am betrothed now, and it wouldn't do to flirt with anyone else."

"Well then, you may flirt all you want with Aimee, for she shall be there, you know. Indeed, it is too bad she promised to see her great aunt at dinner today, for you could have started flirting with her now."

"Flirt with Aimee?" The thought caught him up short. He put his hand over the pocket that contained her miniature, and felt oddly uncertain. How did one flirt with a goddess? He thought he remembered, long ago, teasing Aimee when he had first met her, but she was different now, not really a young girl, but a woman, queenly in bearing and beautiful. A man did not tease and flirt with such a woman but worshiped at her feet. Other, lesser women might be worth a smile or a tease, but Aimee, he was sure, was above such common behavior. Or . . . or was that just her portrait? He tried to think of Aimee as he had seen her earlier this day, but saw only the miniature in its frame.

Psyche gazed at him curiously. "But of course! You were used to do that a great deal before you left for the army some years ago. Do you not remember?"

It seemed an age ago—if he had really done such a

thing. He remembered kissing her, or perhaps it was a dream, for he could not imagine how he could have been so bold. Scenes from battles, of blood and sweat, rose up in his mind and the comparison between such dirt that had surrounded him and the purity that surrounded Aimee was obscene. He could not have done such a thing. He shook his head.

"You must remember!" Psyche said, looking at him curiously. "Why, she was forever blushing because of your teasing. Indeed, I often wondered why she put up with you."

Kenneth pulled out Aimee's miniature from his pocket and smiled at it. "Because she has the patience of a saint," he said. "If I teased her as you say, I must have been an absolute brute." He sighed. It all went to show how perfect his betrothed was. He raised his eyes to see Psyche and his mother exchange worried looks.

Lady Hathaway gazed at him anxiously. "Perhaps I should get a restorative of some sort. Are you sure you did not suffer some sort of head injury, Kenneth? I believe persons who have suffered such blows lose their memories. Or no—! It must be the fever you had—it must have affected your brain."

Kenneth burst out laughing. "Lord no, Mother! I would have known if I'd been head-injured, and my fever wasn't as bad as that." He shook his head and sighed. "A great deal has happened but the worst that I've felt lately is tired and hungry. And since I've eaten enough to fill three men, the latter has been dealt with."

"But tired!" cried Lady Hathaway. "I should have guessed! You must retire immediately, love, and rest."

Psyche rolled her eyes at her brother, and Kenneth laughed. "Don't worry, Mother, truly. I'll be all right and tight in the morning."

Lady Hathaway continued to hover and look at him

anxiously for the rest of his stay, and this made him doubly determined not to stay at home but find his own lodgings. It was bad enough that he tended to get into arguments with his father, but to have his mother hovering about him made him want to twitch and do something outrageous.

At last the dinner was over, and Kenneth heaved a sigh of relief as he stepped out into the evening. A small smile grew on his face as he walked away from his family's house. Outrageous. Perhaps that was the problem behind his . . . malaise, was the word he'd prefer to use to describe it, though it was a damned weakling word to use for a soldier. He remembered the larks he'd get up to when he'd be bored out of his mind between battles. He'd always felt more alive, more energetic afterward. Perhaps he could find Bertie Garthwaite and see if he was up to any fun, or maybe they'd have a look in at White's or Jackson's boxing saloon.

Anything was better than the confusion he'd felt whenever he thought of Aimee.

Psyche caught her mother glancing at her for the third time within a half hour as they sat together quietly in the drawing room, that evening after Kenneth had left. It was Friday, and they had decided to rest, for they had gone out almost every evening to some rout, ball, or musicale, and when Psyche had hesitated at yet another invitation last week, Lady Hathaway had decided that it could not hurt to have at least one day of the week that was not caught up in some vigorous entertainment. They had invited Aimee to stay with them and have a comfortable coze, but she was still with her elderly great-aunt that evening, for the poor woman was quite fragile and weak. Once again Lady Hathaway glanced at Psyche, and this time she bit her lower lip as well.

Psyche put her embroidery down on her lap. "What is it, Mama? You have been casting me looks time and time again this last half hour."

Lady Hathaway sighed. "Perhaps I am merely overly anxious. Did . . . did Kenneth seem a little different to you this evening?"

"Different—how?" Psyche said cautiously. "He seems a little leaner than he was when he was younger, but since he seems quite healthy and seems to have grown, too, I doubt it is anything remarkable."

"No, it is not that, of course," Lady Hathaway said, waving her hand dismissively. "No, it is . . . I suppose it is that odd way he has of speaking of Aimee. To be sure, he sounds very devoted, which is as it should be. But he looked completely besotted, the way he gazed at that miniature of her. It made me positively uncomfortable, for he had never looked so—well, I dislike to say it of my only son, but he looked quite idiotic. I cannot wish any child of mine to look so in public." She frowned. "Perhaps I am refining too much on the matter—you have seen him with Aimee, child; did he behave as he ought?"

Psyche hesitated. What could she say? She supposed he must have, and yet Aimee had seemed uneasy with him. "It is difficult to say, Mama," she said at last. "I know he has not done anything he should not have, for he was very proper and *extremely* respectful of Aimee."

There was a dissatisfied look on Lady Hathaway's face. "I suppose they did nothing untoward. But poor Aimee is a shy young lady, and I cannot think an extreme respect would do anything except make her feel more uncomfortable than she already is in society. I had counted on Kenneth to help escort—yes, and there! He talked of escorting *you* to balls but he said nothing about Aimee!"

"Very unnatural of him, of course, Mama," Psyche said, and grinned.

Her mother tried to look stern but laughed. "Heavens, Psyche! I suppose I should be grateful he agreed to attend any female at a ball at all. But you know what I mean. I half expected him to refuse to escort you because of a prior engagement with Aimee. But he mentioned nothing of the sort! It is almost as if he had forgotten her altogether—except when he gazed at that portrait. And even then he did not mention anything about squiring her about town." Lady Hathaway paused for a moment while a speculative gleam appeared in her eye. "After all, it could not hurt to bring Aimee a little bit more into fashion. Not that she is a dowd, of course! But there is such a thing as excessive modesty, and certainly you cannot say Aimee is at the forefront of fashion. Especially if one were to compare her to a Frenchwoman, which I am sure Kenneth has seen from time to time. While I cannot like anyone under my care to look like a Frenchwoman, you must admit they have a certain flair." Lady Hathaway frowned for a moment. "What do you think, my dear? Do you think it would be a good thing to bring Aimee to look a little more à la mode?"

"It certainly cannot hurt, Mama," Psyche said. She shifted uneasily in her seat and took up her embroidery again. The idea that Harry had made a mistake again and caused Kenneth to fall in love with the portrait instead of Aimee had definitely occurred to her, but it was not something she thought Mama would understand. She was not sure how she would explain it for one thing, and then explaining Harry—She shuddered. No, Mama would definitely not understand. Mama only knew of Harry as an imaginary childhood playmate. Psyche took in a deep breath. In all the years Harry had been with her, she had learned discretion, at least.

"And," she continued, "Kenneth has just come home, and I daresay he is not used to being in England after being away for so long. Perhaps he will change once he settles into civilian life."

Her mother cast her a doubtful look. "I hope so." Her face cleared and she smiled. "However, he is a good boy, and I know he will not do anything so scandalous as to jilt her. He is *very* honorable, after all."

Psyche nodded and bent her head to her work again. But she did not feel as confident as her mother sounded. Honor was all very well, but it did not particularly make one happy. Why, look at Lord Wellington! He was certainly an honorable man, but it was rumored that neither he nor Kitty Pakenham were particularly happy. For all that Kenneth liked to tease and could be horridly annoying, she did want him and Aimee to be happy. Then, too, she remembered Kenneth's tricks and the wild pranks he used to play before he went into the army and wondered if the army had totally obliterated this tendency from his nature . . . she rather doubted it.

She held her embroidery closer to the light and gazed at the pattern of hearts and birds upon it. A brief shadow passed over it, and she looked up at her mother and smiled.

"Very pretty, love!" Lady Hathaway said. "Have you decided to what you will apply it?"

"I think I will turn it into a counterpane—a wedding gift for Kenneth and Aimee." Psyche gazed intently at one side of the embroidery frame, frowned, and let out a small growl. "Oh, fiddlesticks! I have misstitched this heart and it's missing a piece."

Lady Hathaway patted her shoulder. "You have better eyes than I—I can hardly see it. But you are such a good needlewoman, I know you will correct it."

Psyche smiled at her mother and set herself to undoing the heart she had stitched. She thought of the look upon Aimee's face when she and Kenneth had left—a bereft, lost look—and wished she could stitch up real hearts just as easily.

She shook her head at herself. Perhaps she was refining too much on the matter. Perhaps all would be well and Aimee was just as sure of Kenneth's affection as she always was.

She remembered the confused look on Kenneth's face when he was at Aimee's house and again at dinner, and she was not all that sure, herself. Psyche set another stitch and bit her lip. Perhaps it would be a good thing to ask Aimee along to their outings so that Kenneth would remember what it was like to be with his betrothed again. She liked Aimee very well for she was her dear friend, and certainly she would not like her to be hurt.

But she could not help thinking that Kenneth should have thought of inviting Aimee first.

# Chapter 3

It was daylight. Kenneth Hathaway knew it was by the way the sunlight struck his eyes and turned his eyelids red on the insides. He turned over and groaned. For all that he'd been used to long marches, he was not used to the late hours London society kept and though he was almost as strict as a Methodist with regard to spirits, the two glasses of gin an army friend had persuaded him to drink at the gaming hell did not help make him feel particularly lively this morning.

No, afternoon. It must be afternoon—early afternoon, for his window faced west and there was the sun blazing quite brightly through it. Quickly he got out of bed. "Jackson!" he roared toward the chamber door, and strode to his wardrobe.

Devil take it! Five days ago—or had it been a week?—he had promised Aimee he'd call upon her this afternoon. He should have asked Jackson to wake him, but he must have forgotten. He paused before the wardrobe and pressed the palms of his hands against his eyes. God, he was still tired. Would he never stop feeling tired?

"Jackson!" he called again and opened his wardrobe. The chamber door opened with a bang and his batman—now valet—limped in.

"Sir?" the man said, standing at attention. He was a

somewhat plump man, dressed very neatly, his homely face still appealing despite a scar across his nose.

"Good man," Kenneth said. "Prompt, this time. But don't bang the damned door. We don't live in a tent anymore and flinging doors about is not according to regulations here."

"Yes, sir!" Jackson said respectfully. He held out two starched lengths of cloth. "Your neckcloths, sir."

"Excellent! Put them over there." Kenneth pointed to the bed. "Carefully. And I'll need to shave."

"Certainly, sir!"

It had been fortuitous that he'd run into the man some days ago as he as going to headquarters. Jackson had been a good man while they were in Spain, a good sergeant, a soldier any officer would want by his side. But the man had lost a finger and part of his foot, and could not find any work when he returned. He'd been down to his last groat when Kenneth had seen him and he'd hired the man on the spot. Damned shame what happened to good soldiers after a war. Kenneth gritted his teeth at the thought. Discarded like rubbish once they'd done their duty.

He drew in his breath and pushed aside the memories of men wounded and dead, and splashed lukewarm water over his face from the washbasin sitting in the sun. He grabbed a towel and wiped off his face, then caught sight of himself in the mirror. He looked old. His face was brown and weathered, and there were tiny wrinkles around his eyes from squinting into the hot Spanish sun.

He was only four-and-twenty years of age, hardly old. It was just that he hadn't had a shave yet, that was all, and he was tired from staying up so late. And he was right, for after Jackson had shaved him and helped him with his clothes, he felt a little better.

It was sunny out of doors, and this time he was able to

ignore the cries of street sellers and the rumble of carts
and carriages. He shivered a little, and wished he had
worn a thicker coat, though it seemed the people walking
and driving about the streets felt the chill not at all. Perhaps it was the contrast between Spain's heat and the gray
skies of London that had brought him down—he was not
used to it, or the relative chilliness of England's climate.
He would become used to it soon, certainly.

"Hathaway!"

Kenneth turned swiftly and spied a tall, thin young
man with a shock of blond hair who was coming toward
him. "By God, Bertram—Bertie—Garthwaite! I haven't
seen you in—"

"Donkey's years," Bertie said, grinning, and clapped
him on the shoulder.

"Not that long!"

"Been so busy with Bonaparte, you've forgotten how
long, I'll wager."

Kenneth smiled wryly. "I suppose it has been busy.
Now that the man's off to Elba, I'm able to catch up with
everyone."

"Much to catch up on, I imagine." Bertie nodded
wisely. "What say you come along with me to Gunter's?
I'm fair gut-foundered right now, starving to death."

Kenneth laughed. "I see you haven't got rid of your in-
testinal infestation yet."

Bertie gave him a disgusted look. "Dash it all, Hathaway, I never had one! Or if I did, that Blue Ruin you
dumped down my throat when we were at Cambridge got
rid of it." But he grinned. "Can't help if it takes a lot to
keep me going. Well, just look at me!" He spread out his
arms.

"Tall as a church steeple, that's you, Bertie," Kenneth
said. He hesitated, thinking of the food to be had at
Gunter's and his stomach rumbled persuasively. He hadn't

had any breakfast, and it wasn't all that late in the afternoon. It would be damned annoying to have one's stomach rumble throughout the afternoon.

"*Ices,*" Bertie said in a low, portentous voice, obviously noting Kenneth's hesitation.

Ices. He hadn't had that for a long time. He remembered the heat and exhaustion during his stay in Spain and how his mouth had felt gritty with dust and dryness . . . the thought of cold sweet ices. . . .

He grinned, snapped his heels together, and smartly saluted his friend. "Gunter's it is," he said, and they walked companionably down the street.

Aimee glanced at the drawing-room clock once again, and noted with despair that only five minutes had passed since she last looked. Perhaps she had mistaken the time, or perhaps Kenneth had . . . She was sure his note had said early in the afternoon, but here it was two o'clock already, and there was no sign of him. Could he have forgotten? Surely not! He had never forgotten to meet her before. She looked down at the embroidery she was stitching. It needed only a few more stitches and it would be done.

But another half hour passed, her stitchery was complete, and there was no knock on the door. It had been five days since she had seen Kenneth last. Slowly Aimee rose from her chair and proceeded to go up to her chambers. There was a ball tonight that she had thought she'd decline, thinking that her visit with Kenneth would be a long one and would make it difficult to prepare for it. But he had not arrived, and she was not one to stay idle. She might as well prepare for the ball.

But before she reached the door, a knock sounded and Aimee's heart leapt—it must be Kenneth!

It was not. The butler bowed as he opened the door. "Lieutenant Francis Pargeter-Hathaway, Miss."

Aimee bit her lip, then nodded. Kenneth did not like the lieutenant—he thought it presumptuous for the lieutenant to use the Hathaway name—but other than that, Aimee could not find much to fault in him. The lieutenant had returned before Kenneth by about a month and had made himself a name amongst the *ton*. He was definitely a dandy, and after reading of all the hardships Kenneth had suffered during his campaigns, she wondered how Mr. Pargeter could have wished to have joined the army. However, he had always claimed a dance whenever they happened to be at a ball together, and seemed pleasant enough.

She sighed as he entered, for her heart did a little leap before the depression that always followed Lieutenant Pargeter's entrance. There was a marked resemblance between him and Kenneth, and it always made her heart ache a little to see the similarities. As the lieutenant bowed over her hand, she could not help marking how he was of the same height and build, and how his lean face was similar in structure to Kenneth's. But she looked at his green eyes that were very unlike her betrothed's and at his hair, a much lighter red than Kenneth's auburn. His nose was more straight than Kenneth's, which should have made the lieutenant more classically handsome . . . but she did not find him so somehow. Certainly he was better dressed, for Kenneth was sometimes careless of his clothes and was not above looking rumpled from time to time. It was something she had often thought was an endearing trait, that Kenneth thought more of her than the cut of his clothes.

But the lieutenant was pleasant enough, and while she had waited for Kenneth's return, she sometimes imagined

Mr. Francis Pargeter was Kenneth, and for a short time she was content.

"My dear lady," Mr. Pargeter said and smiled into her eyes. "Dare I hope that you can come with me in my carriage to Hyde Park this afternoon?"

Aimee pulled her hand from his grasp, smiled, and shook her head. "I am sorry, but I have another engagement. Kenneth said he would come see me this afternoon, you see, and I am waiting for him."

Mr. Pargeter's brows rose. "Indeed? How odd." He took out his quizzing glass and gazed at the clock on the mantelpiece with it.

"Odd? How can it be odd that I am to see him?"

He turned to her again and smiled, swinging his quizzing glass lazily upon its chain. "Only that I saw him with Bertie Garthwaite at Gunter's but a few minutes ago."

Aimee felt suddenly cold and alone, but she shook her head and smiled. "No doubt he stopped for a moment and will soon come here. So you see, I need to wait only a little longer."

"And yet I overheard them talking of walking to Jackson's saloon just before I left. Perhaps I was mistaken," Mr. Pargeter said thoughtfully.

Aimee lifted her chin and stared at the lieutenant. "No doubt you were," she said. "Kenneth has not forgotten an appointment with me yet."

"There is always a first time," Mr. Pargeter drawled. "Are you sure you would not consider a drive with me to Hyde Park? The afternoon is pleasant, you know, even though it is almost over."

"No, you are very kind, but no." There was a slight mournful tilt to the man's mouth, and Aimee relented a little. "But if you wish, you may stay for some tea, and . . . and if Kenneth does not arrive in fifteen minutes, perhaps I can go out with you for a little while."

Mr. Pargeter smiled widely and bowed over her hand again. "How kind of you, ma'am." He sat in the chair she indicated and she pulled the bell rope and asked the servant who answered to bring some refreshments.

Aimee was surprised to find that the time went quickly, more quickly than she had anticipated. She had not talked at much length with Mr. Pargeter, but it turned out he was a good conversationalist and knew all the gossip about town. Her eyes widened at some of his anecdotes, and she could not help blushing at some of the indiscretions he had related regarding certain members of the *ton*. But he was a sophisticated man . . . she supposed such subjects were often talked of in society. Things were quite different from the country, to be sure!

The clock struck the half hour, startling her, and when Mr. Pargeter rose and held out his hand, she stared at him for a moment.

"Our carriage ride, ma'am?" he asked, smiling slightly.

Aimee looked at the clock and saw that fifteen minutes had indeed passed. She bit back a sigh and suppressed the surge of disappointment because Kenneth had not come as he had promised. She smiled at Mr. Pargeter instead and nodded.

"Very well, sir. I shall need to go up and put on my pelisse, if you would be so kind as to wait."

The lieutenant bowed over her hand again. "Of course," he said.

Aimee walked slowly up the stairs to her chambers. She could not help wanting to wait a bit longer—she so wished that Kenneth would come! But she had said she would wait fifteen minutes and so she had. A little anger began to burn inside her chest . . . why did Kenneth not come? He had said he would, and if Mr. Pargeter had not told her that her betrothed was with Bertie Garthwaite, she would have been ill with worry for Kenneth. She hastened her steps and soon she was at her room and quickly pulled on the pelisse her maid had brought out for her.

When she descended again, Mr. Pargeter's admiring gaze could not help but act as a balm upon her disappointment in Kenneth's failure to appear. She lifted her chin, then smiled at the lieutenant. It *was* gratifying to be admired and attended to. Other ladies did not have to wait upon their fiancés for entertainment; there was no reason why she should not enjoy a simple drive in the park with another gentleman than Kenneth.

"I am afraid Miss Mattingly is not in, Miss Hathaway," the butler said, when Psyche came home from the draper's.

Psyche frowned. "That is odd, Trimble. I was sure she would be here, and my brother also." She had purposely dallied at the shop, hoping to give her brother and Aimee some time alone together.

Trimble's expression turned suddenly wooden. "Miss Mattingly has gone out with Lieutenant Pargeter-Hathaway, and Captain Hathaway has not arrived." He opened the door wider. "However, I expect them to return in a few minutes if you wish to wait for them."

"Thank you, Trimble. And that's Pargeter, not Pargeter-Hathaway," Psyche said automatically. Her frown grew deeper. "But I was sure she would be here! I know Kenneth was to call upon her. This is not like Aimee at all." She looked upon the watch pinned upon the bodice of her pelisse and shook her head. "He should have arrived by now." She gazed curiously at the butler. "And I think by your expression that something has happened about which you do not approve."

The butler's face turned even more wooden as he took

the bonnet she gave him. "I do not comment upon my superiors, Miss," he said and looked down his nose at the maid who had come with Psyche into the hall.

She turned to the maid and smiled. "You may go belowstairs, Gwennie." The maid cast an anxious glance at the butler and walked quickly away.

"Ah! Something did happen," Psyche said after the maid had left. "What is it?"

"Far be it from me to—"

"Never mind that, Trimble!" she said, following him to the drawing room. "Aimee will be part of our family in a very short time, so I shall know about it soon, I daresay. You might as well tell me."

A gloomy look replaced the wooden one. "I have cause to wonder if such a felicitous event will occur."

"Nonsense!" Psyche stepped into the drawing room—indeed empty—and sat down upon a sofa near the fireplace. "They are very much in love and are betrothed. Of course they will marry."

Silence ensued. Psyche watched curiously as the butler's face almost writhed with emotion: from gloom to severity to an acute anxiety. It was almost painful to watch how he tried to control the obvious strong feelings regarding his stature as butler and equally strong feelings of disapproval. She almost dismissed him to save him the struggle, but he finally burst out, "Miss Hathaway, I have heard the captain has gone to Gunter's with Bertie Garthwaite instead of calling upon Miss Aimee."

"Ah!" Psyche said.

"Not that I would ever eavesdrop, Miss Hathaway!"

"No, of course not, Trimble. You were merely doing your duty by keeping yourself informed of the family's activities," Psyche said kindly.

The butler breathed a sigh of relief. "Miss Aimee was

not pleased, miss. And I could hardly blame her for wishing for a bit of entertainment on a bright day like this."

"Naturally," Psyche said. She looked up and smiled at the butler. "If you would be so kind as to bring me a little tea, I would be very grateful."

"Of course, miss," Trimble replied and breathed another sigh of relief before he left the room.

Psyche shook her head. Something had gone awry, and very badly at that. Kenneth never had missed an appointment with Aimee before, and he had never delayed in being with her that she had heard of. There had not been a quarrel, so that could not be the reason behind his apparent reluctance. And yet, there seemed to be an odd reticence about her brother when it came to Aimee. She smiled at Trimble when he brought the tea, then nibbled on a sweet biscuit contemplatively. Kenneth's actions were at complete odds with the fervent adoration he seemed to have for Aimee whenever he spoke of her or looked at her portrait. Perhaps . . . perhaps Harry should not have shot Kenneth after all. A portrait was not the same as one's beloved, to be sure!

"Psyche."

She jumped, almost upsetting her tea, and turned around. "Heavens, Harry, I *told* you I did not like it when you surprise me like that!" She looked up at her friend indignantly.

Harry grinned and gazed at her, his head cocked to one side. "But you startle delightfully! You don't precisely jump, you know, not like other people do. You sort of bounce, I think."

"Bounce!" Psyche gazed at him severely. "You make me sound like a ball—and I do not think I like that comparison! It seems too . . . too . . ."

"Spherical?" Harry said helpfully. "Round, perhaps?"

"Oh!" Psyche cried, and threw a pillow at him. "You are *horrid*!"

He neatly dodged the pillow and put on an injured look. "But I think roundness is thoroughly enchanting! How can I be horrid for thinking that?"

She felt her face grow hot and she pressed her hands to her cheeks. "Ohhh! See if I speak to you ever again!"

He came around the sofa and sat beside her. "But you shall, you know, because I can see already that you are curious about my new clothes." He crossed his legs and leaned back into the seat cushions and looked as satisfied as a cat in cream.

He was, indeed, dressed differently. His Greek kilt-like chiton was gone: a fine blue jacket was neatly fitted across his shoulders instead, and an impeccably tied neckcloth around his neck. A gold-chased waistcoat peeked from underneath it, and his legs were encased in pale yellow pantaloons. And his wings . . . his wings were gone. Psyche gazed at him, at the way he grinned at her mischievously yet had a hopeful questioning look in his eyes, and she felt an odd twisting sensation in her chest. She glanced away. She was not used to him without his wings and was not sure she liked it.

His hand touched her arm briefly and she looked up at him. His gaze was concerned, though he still smiled. "Is there something the matter?" he asked. "Perhaps I am not dressed in the proper mode?" His expression turned slightly anxious and it occurred to her suddenly that perhaps he wished to please her a little. She smiled at the notion. What nonsense! Harry rarely pleased anyone but himself. It was the way of the Greek gods, after all.

Psyche shook her head and laughed. "You look very well—and there! You have made me compliment you, so I hope your vanity is satisfied."

"You are pleased, then?"

She looked at him, startled. "Why, yes, I suppose so . . . although why you should wish to please me, I don't know. Unless . . ." She gazed at him suspiciously. "Have you been doing something you ought not?"

Harry looked offended. "I? No! And why should I not wish to please you from time to time? Are we not friends?"

"Yes, of course we are," Psyche said instantly, feeling oddly relieved. "But there have been times when you've *wheedled*, you know, and it's because you've done something you should not."

He gave her a triumphant smile. "There, my point exactly. I would not do that if I did not wish to be in your good graces."

Psyche almost asked him why he wished to be in her good graces . . . but then the tolling of the clock caught her attention and made her remember her earlier thoughts and wonder why Harry had such an uneasy air about him.

"Hmph!" she said, and gazed at him speculatively. "What I wonder is if you had noticed anything odd about Kenneth."

He looked uncomfortable and hesitated before he said, "I am not sure, but I have thought perhaps I have made a bit of a mistake regarding your brother, and was hoping to catch him here with Aimee."

"A mistake?" Psyche gazed at her friend anxiously. Was he ill, perhaps? He had never admitted to a mistake so readily before. She took his hand and patted it. "Are . . . are you well, Harry?"

An astonished look crossed his face, then he smiled crookedly, as if he wasn't sure whether to laugh or protest. "By the gods, Psyche, just because I say I might have made a mistake does not mean I feel ill! I have admitted it any number of times."

Psyche smiled skeptically at him and silently ticked off the fingers of one hand.

"Oh, very well! Not often! But at least I am becoming better at it—did I not admit it now, and fairly quickly, too?" He shrugged his shoulders when she only continued to smile at him but said nothing. "At any rate, I think perhaps I should shoot another arrow at your brother, this time in Aimee's presence." He glanced away from her and bit into a biscuit he had selected. "You see . . . I think he might have fallen in love with her portrait, not with her."

"Wellll . . ." Psyche gnawed on her lower lip. "You know I do not like such things and would prefer you do not intervene. Perhaps if I bring it to Kenneth's attention that he is neglecting Aimee, he will remedy it himself. It is not as if you had shot more than one arrow into him, as you did with my brother-in-law."

"I knew you would bring up Blytheland," Harry said, sounding put out. "If I had got to him sooner, it would have solved things more smoothly, I admit it! This is why I wish to remedy my mistake as soon as I can with Kenneth."

She could see the reasoning behind this. Slowly, she nodded. "Very well," she said. A thought struck her and she beamed at him. "I know! Perhaps I can help you."

He looked at her warily. "Help?"

"Wouldn't it be better if both of us tried to shoot Kenneth?"

"I think not."

"Oh, please let me! And I need not know how to draw a bow, because Papa told me a story once in which you used darts, too, and I know I will be able to throw them far better than shooting arrows." She smiled at him in her most persuasive manner.

Harry grimaced. "You know about those, do you?" He

sighed. "I have seen you throw darts. I don't think you are all that accurate with them."

"*That* was many years ago, and I am much better at it now," Psyche said triumphantly. "And think how much more efficient it would be!"

"Well . . ." Harry stared at her for a moment, as if in deep consideration. A sparkle seemed to gleam in his eyes. "When do you suppose they might next meet?"

"Let's see . . . it's Tuesday now . . . I suppose it would be next week, Wednesday, at Almack's."

He suddenly rose and turned away from her and seemed to be attacked by a series of hiccups, then began to cough violently. Psyche rushed to him and pounded him on his back until he stopped.

"Are you feeling well, Harry?" she asked anxiously.

He drew in a deep breath and let it out again, then turned to her. His face was flushed, but his attack of coughing must not have been very serious, for he was smiling slightly. He patted her hand that she had placed on his arm.

"Oh, I am quite well," he replied cheerfully. "It must have been a fragment of biscuit in my throat." The mischievous sparkle was in his eyes again, and Psyche could not help feeling a little uneasy. "Yes, you are right, Psyche. I think it would be very am—efficient if you were to throw darts at Kenneth, too. And Almack's would be the best place, for he would be obliged to dance with Aimee, after all, and what would be a better opportunity than that?"

This time it was Psyche's turn to eye him warily. "You are agreeing to it very quickly. I think perhaps you are up to some mischief."

"I?" Harry placed a hand upon his chest and looked at her with wide, innocent eyes. "I promise you, I shall not shoot at anyone but Kenneth, and you know well enough that I am an accurate shot."

Psyche stared at him, gnawing on her lower lip in consideration. "You promise, do you?"

"True blue and will never stain," he said promptly, using an oath she had taught him when they were children. "Not only that, but I will give you as many darts as you wish."

She could not help feeling there was something Harry was keeping from her, but he had promised her he would shoot only at Kenneth, and he always kept his promises. And there was nothing else in his agreement she could fault.

"Very well," she said, and offered him the plate of biscuits again.

He shook his head and rose from the sofa. "No, thank you, I think I need to go and make up some darts. Perhaps you should make certain that Kenneth goes to Almack's. It seems he has forgotten his appointment with Aimee—if so, I think we cannot depend on him to remember to attend Almack's."

Psyche nodded. "True. He doesn't really like to go, after all, and I have found it very easy to forget to do things if I don't like to do them." She smiled up at Harry. "It's very kind of you to let me throw darts, too." She took his hand and squeezed it.

He shrugged and grinned at her. "Not at all, not at all," he said carelessly. He moved from her and slowly began to shimmer and disappear. "You wished to help, after all," he whispered close to her ear. And then he was gone.

Psyche stared at the spot where he had been. She still felt a little uneasy . . . but she would be at Almack's after all, and could watch him. She pulled the bell rope for Trimble and when he arrived instructed him to leave a message for Aimee upon her return. But just as she was about to go upstairs to change her clothes, the uneasiness suddenly flowered and she almost stopped in her tracks.

Almack's! Oh, dear. How was Harry to get in? He had no voucher or ticket to enter, and even if he were to use his invisibility to pass Mr. Willis at the staircase, she was sure none of the patronesses would recognize him. What if he were to be thrown out of the assembly rooms? It would be very embarrassing, and she was not at all sure that Harry would not exact some sort of revenge upon whatever patroness demanded his ejection. A god could do dreadful things if angered.

A vision of Mrs. Drummond-Burrell transformed into a cow in the middle of the assembly room rose before Psyche's eyes and made her shudder. Perhaps she should deny any acquaintance with Harry if such a thing should happen. She did not like to do such a cowardly thing, but she could not help thinking that introducing a cow into the hallowed halls of Almack's would bar one from getting vouchers forever, even if the cow happened to be one of the patronesses. And how would she explain that to Mama?

Psyche quickly ran up the stairs. She would try to call out to Harry once she returned to her room, and tell him they could not do it at Almack's. It would not work at all! It would be much better if they delayed it and went to Lady Connington's ball. It would be much easier to introduce him as a friend of the family's, and she would be supported in this by Cassandra, for she had seen Harry, too, before she was married and a few times since then.

But when she stepped into her room and called for Harry, he did not appear. Psyche's uneasiness grew. Well, perhaps it would not be all that bad. If Harry could not get into Almack's or was made to leave the rooms, it would all come to naught anyway, and certainly she could persuade him not to take vengeance upon anyone if he were ejected. Harry did say he wished to please her, after all. Psyche gnawed her lower lip, then sighed. One never could predict what would happen with Harry about.

However, it would not hurt to have Kenneth there. At the very least she could make sure he and Aimee had more opportunities to meet. She called for her maid again, ordered a coach, and pulled on her pelisse and bonnet. Trimble had said that Kenneth had gone to Gunter's with Bertie Garthwaite. Very well, then! She would seek him out and make sure he would attend Almack's. She remembered Aimee's confused eyes the last time she had spoken of Kenneth, and imagined the disappointment she must have felt when he did not come today to see her.

Psyche pressed her lips together firmly as she descended the stairs to the waiting coach. At the very least she would give her brother a piece of her mind!

Gunter's shop at Number Seven Berkeley Square was filled with customers and busy as usual. The afternoon was sunny and calling upon one's friends and relations an exhausting task on a day such as this; anyone who was anyone knew that Gunter's was the best place for one to refresh oneself.

As Kenneth strolled toward the shop, he could see an intense preoccupation growing upon Bertie's face. The man was no doubt listening intently to the orders given by the ladies in their coaches to Gunter's waiters—and so it was, for as they came close to one of them, Bertie cocked his head and his brows furrowed with even more concentration. Then he nodded, smiled, and led the way into the shop.

He watched as Bertie caught the eye of a waiter who hastily led them to a booth in a quiet corner.

"Tea, with some lemon biscuits to start, sir?" said the

waiter respectfully. Kenneth hid a grin. Obviously his friend was well known here.

Bertie smiled and nodded. "Yes. Turtle soup after that, with some lobster patties—I assume you have lobster patties today?"

The waiter looked a little anxious. "We made sure to have more of them made especially after the last time you were here, sir. I hope they will suffice."

Bertie waved a dismissing hand. "Never mind that. If you don't have enough, I'll order something else. Let's see . . . I think I'll have some slices of Portuguese ham, Jamaican bananas—and if you don't have those, some dried peaches will do—and then I overheard Lady Sandringham mentioning small cakes with brandied cherries. . . ."

The list went on, and Kenneth wondered privately if Bertie was going to eat it all. How his friend could be so thin and yet eat so much had always been a mystery to him. Perhaps he carried what was left over in his pockets and saved it for later. And yet, his coat was stretched tight over his shoulders and his very flat stomach; no pocket could contain whatever might be left over from such a feast as Bertie was ordering. It was clearly a worrisome thing at least to the waiter; the poor man looked very relieved when Kenneth only ordered an ice.

However, Kenneth was rather glad he had agreed to come to Gunter's with Bertie. He hadn't had ices in a long time, and then there were the other sweets that were offered. Well, after being deprived so long of them, you couldn't blame a man for sampling more than a few. And he hadn't remembered how much Bertie could consume at a table. Not one crumb was left on their plates and now his friend was eyeing the comestibles at the next table as if he were about to pounce on them.

"I never knew you were in the army, Bertie," Kenneth said.

Bertie pulled his gaze away from a laden platter carried by a waiter going to another table. "I? The army?" He frowned. "Noble cause and all for King and country, but I was never as army mad as you."

"Thing was, I'd always hear of food and supplies coming our way, but they never appeared. Now I know. You secretly joined the army, waylaid the supply train, and ate all the rations before we could get to them."

"I don't eat *that* much!"

Kenneth eyed the empty plates on the table and grinned. "Seems to me you ate as much as an army could hold right here."

"It wasn't as if you didn't—"

"Kenneth!" cried a female voice.

He turned and saw Psyche coming toward him accompanied by her maid. "What *are* you doing here?"

"Psyche! I'm having a bit to eat with Bertie here, obviously. It's too bad you didn't come earlier—we could have sat together." Psyche turned to her maid and instructed her to go home now that she was with her brother.

Bertie rose and bowed elegantly. "Pleased to see you, Miss Psyche. Will I see you at Almack's, and may I hope for a dance if you are going?"

"Why yes, I will be there and will be happy to dance with you," Psyche said smiling at Bertie, then turned to her brother and frowned. "In fact, I am going with Aimee. Which means *you* had better be there, too, Kenneth."

Kenneth rolled his eyes. "Of course I will—I said I would, didn't I?" An uneasy feeling came over him at the mention of his betrothed's name. Was there something he was supposed to do?

Psyche put her hands on her hips and stared at Kenneth, her eyes narrowing. "I don't see your word as anything to rely on, brother—especially since you were supposed to call upon Aimee this afternoon and have not," she said, her voice low and fierce.

"Oh, no!" Kenneth groaned. "Bertie—devil take it!—sorry to leave like this but I must—" Bertie nodded and waved his hand at him in a dismissing gesture, but when Kenneth turned to leave, Psyche seized his arm.

"You are too late, stupid!" she said angrily. "She has given up and has gone out driving."

"Out?"

"Yes. With Francis Pargeter-Hathaway."

"That's Francis *Pargeter*—damn him!" He pulled away and strode out of the shop, Psyche almost running to keep up with him.

"What the blood—what has he to do with Aimee?"

"Doing what you should be doing, idiot brother! He is giving her the attention that you should have given her—why, how many times have you even seen her since you returned? Hardly any! I have been thinking you have begun not to care for her. You're not a proper beau at all, and I cannot blame Aimee for wishing to look about her a little." Psyche hid her smile. Kenneth's words had come out sharp and biting and now his lips were pressed together tightly. There! Clearly he was jealous and perhaps would pay better attention to Aimee after this.

"Nonsense! I have seen her every day since I have returned."

"How can you say so? I was with her almost all day yesterday, and two days ago, and you never came to see her."

A confused look came over Kenneth's face. "But . . . I am certain I have. Besides, I have her portrait with me at all times, and certainly I have looked at that every day!"

"That is *not* the same as seeing her in person!"

He had taken out the portrait and gazed at it, and his expression became soft and . . . Psyche did not want to admit it of her own brother whom she loved, but he looked quite lack-witted. He had not looked like this before that she could remember. If this was what people looked like when they fell in love, she would rather not do it. It was bad enough for her to have red hair, but to look like an idiot on top of that would be a horrible comedown. Perhaps it was Harry's arrows that made Kenneth look so. Well, in that case, the sooner she and Harry returned him to his original state, the better. She shook his arm, and he pulled his gaze from the portrait and looked at her as if he had just woken up from a deep sleep.

"Do come along, Kenneth! For heaven's sake, you cannot be standing in the middle of the street staring at a portrait! I thought you were going to find Aimee."

A fierce light came into his eyes, and he nodded briskly. "Right you are." He hailed a hackney and Psyche quickly jumped up into it with him.

"Pargeter! How dare he go after Aimee? He isn't fit to touch the hem of her skirt!" Kenneth growled. A thought seemed to strike him and his face grew even more stormy. "And if he dares do anything with her skirts I'll have his head, damn him!"

"Kenneth!" Psyche cried. "Aimee is *not* like that!"

"No, but he is!"

"Nonsense! He seems a perfect gentleman and is accepted everywhere."

" 'Seems' is the word," Kenneth retorted. "He pretended to be as good as a dam—dashed eunuch back in Spain, but I'd heard more than a few rumors about him."

"Rumors!" Psyche sniffed. "Is that all? I am surprised you take gossip for truth."

"He's slippery, and that's no gossip. I wouldn't put it past him to give a lady a slip on the shoulder."

Psyche looked at her brother with interest. "What does that mean—'a slip on the shoulder'?"

"It means—" Kenneth stopped and glared at her. "Never mind!" The hackney rumbled to a stop in front of the Hathaways' house and Kenneth leapt out of it. "I'm taking a horse—there's no way a carriage is going to catch up with them in the afternoon crowd."

"Heavens, Kenneth," Psyche said. "You are acting as if Pargeter has committed some crime, when the only thing he has done is take Aimee out for a carriage ride."

"Damned encroaching worm."

"Well what in heaven's name are you going to do? You can hardly carry her off on your saddlebow!" Psyche tumbled out of the carriage and ran after him into the house.

A strange wild look entered Kenneth's eyes and he grinned fiercely. "Perhaps I will. Trimble!" he roared into the hallway. The butler appeared quickly. "Where did that devil Pargeter go?"

"H-hyde Park, sir. Or so I thought I heard," stuttered the butler.

"Tell one of the grooms to get me a horse. Now!"

"Yes, yes, sir!" the butler said, casting an anxious look at Psyche before he left.

"You can't be serious, Kenneth!"

Her brother laughed. "Just watch me!" He walked out of the hall and out the door again.

"Kenneth!" cried Psyche and ran after him. But he had already mounted the horse brought to him, and her words were lost in the thunder of pounding hooves.

# Chapter 4

The afternoon was still sunny as Aimee and Lieutenant Pargeter wended their way down to Hyde Park in his curricle. She was determined to be glad she'd decided to go on this ride. Lieutenant Pargeter continued telling her of this person or that as they drove, but she could not help feeling a little uncomfortable. He was very amiable to be sure, but he seemed not to be able to stop from commenting about each person they met after they left. His comments were not unpleasant, but somehow they seemed less than flattering. It made her feel uncertain about him, and she could not help wondering what he would say of her once they parted. However, it was certainly better than staying indoors. And yet, Aimee caught herself looking at each red uniform they passed, hoping that it might be Kenneth on his way to see her.

She did not see him. Aimee pressed her lips together. Well, if he could not keep his appointment with her, why should she not enjoy herself? She turned to smile at Mr. Pargeter.

"Do you go to Almack's?" It was rather bold of her to ask it, but the little angry heat that had begun before she had agreed to this outing still burned inside of her.

"Why yes." He gazed at her, and it seemed a warm light came into his eyes. "Dare I hope you might be available for a dance?"

Aimee blushed and looked down at her clasped hands in her lap. He had asked almost before she had finished her question. Perhaps he liked her a little, and that was certainly gratifying after Kenneth's lack of attention lately. "Yes . . . I believe I shall be."

"The first one, perhaps?"

Aimee looked at him, surprised. He should know that the first one should properly be reserved for her betrothed.

"Ah! Forgive me!" Mr. Pargeter smiled ruefully. "I was wishing not long ago that you were not betrothed, and I am afraid the wish came out in my words."

She was not certain what to say. She felt he was too bold, and yet she could not help being flattered. A little yearning part of her felt comforted at his clear wish to be with her . . . as Kenneth did not. Or did he? She remembered Kenneth's worshipful words upon his return home, and Mr. Pargeter's flattering ones. And yet Mr. Pargeter was here, inviting her out for a drive in his carriage, whereas Kenneth was not.

She nodded and smiled. "You are forgiven, even though I suspect you are a terrible flatterer! You may have the second dance, then."

Lieutenant Pargeter smiled into her eyes and raised her hand to his lips. "I am honored," he said.

Aimee sighed. It was *very* pleasant to be sought after for once. Perhaps it would not hurt to see more of Mr. Pargeter from time to time, just for company and conversation, of course.

She smiled at Lieutenant Pargeter again, then glanced away, blushing, for his gaze grew warmer and somehow more intimate, drifting from her face to the base of her throat. It made her want to close the collar of her pelisse closer together, but that was a silly notion—her collar was very high, and there was no décolletage at all. Yet,

she felt quite uncomfortable, somehow. A flash of yellow
caught her distracted gaze—new daffodils to the side of
the road.

"Do you think we could stop for a little while?" she
asked. "Those flowers are quite lovely and I would like
to view them more closely." Perhaps she would not feel
so uncomfortable if she had something to do, like walk
about a bit and look at flowers and shrubbery.

"Of course," Lieutenant Pargeter said, and stopped the
carriage.

It was a little better at first when they got out, but
somehow they seemed to wander very close to some
trees, away from the people who walked or rode about
Hyde Park. Aimee cast a quick, uncomfortable look at the
lieutenant, but he continued chatting of this and that, and
his face was smoothly cordial, revealing nothing but
pleasantness. It was nothing, of course.

But she was quite wrong. As they came into a small
copse of trees, the lieutenant quickly grasped her hand.

"Miss Mattingly—Aimee—I must speak!"

She started, blushed, and tried to pull her hand away.
"Please, Lieutenant, I cannot think what you mean by
this—"

He held her hand firmly. "I have been silent for too
long!"

"I doubt that!" Aimee said breathlessly, still tugging.
"You have been speaking at length for the last half hour
about everyone we have met. I can hardly suppose you to
be without words now." She pulled as hard as she could,
and her hand slipped from out her glove, but he grasped
her arm instead.

She glanced at him, and for one moment a bit of fear
struck her as a black, angry look flashed across his face.
But it was gone, and she thought she must have imagined
it, since he was smiling now.

"You jest, of course," he replied. "But you must hear me—Aimee, I have come under your spell—"

"Stop!" she cried. "You forget yourself! I am betrothed, as well you know, and I certainly have not given you permission to use my Christian name. Stop at once!" Her heart beat fast with both embarrassment and fear. Heaven help her if anyone should see her like this with the lieutenant!

He held her hand tighter. "You must listen—"

"No, please!" Her heart hammered harder, until it seemed that it pounded through her whole body, and she could feel it down to the soles of her feet. Suddenly Lieutenant Pargeter's face blenched, his eyes seemed almost to start from their sockets, and he let go of her hand so quickly that she stumbled.

"What—?" Aimee cried, and her heart pounded even harder—or no, it could not be her heart, for the ground trembled beneath her feet to a different rhythm. She looked at the lieutenant and saw he was staring not at her, but beyond. Quickly she turned.

A flame-haired demon upon a frothing horse pounded down upon them. No, it was not a demon, but a man, dressed in red regimentals. His face was pale and a fierce smile was fixed upon his lips. Oh, heavens, it was Kenneth!

A small moan issued from Lieutenant Pargeter's lips. "Oh, God!" he cried. "Not here! He's mad! I never thought he'd—" But his words were cut off by the thunder of hooves and his panicked dash into a tall bush.

Suddenly the breath in Aimee's lungs left her as a strong arm swept her up from where she stood. She gasped frantically for air, and gained it only to gasp again when her hip slapped against the hard leather saddle in front of her betrothed. The wind buffeted her bonnet, pushing the brim over her eyes so that she could see nothing but a papiêr maché cherry that had come loose from her hat and bounced on her nose with each gallop of the horse.

At last she managed to breathe. "Kenneth!" she cried. The horse continued to gallop and Kenneth's arm around her waist held her tighter than ever. She took in a deep breath. "Kenneth!" she shouted. "For heaven's sake, put me down!"

The horse slowed and stopped at last, though Kenneth still held her tightly against him. She wriggled upon the saddle until she could sit a little straighter, her face flushing hot with mortification and anger. Her legs dangled to one side of the horse and she could feel her dress hiked up almost to her knees, showing her legs in a most disgraceful manner. She pushed her bonnet away from her face and tried to push down her skirts as well, but one leg was too tightly wedged against Kenneth's thigh to move properly. Embarrassment rose hotly from her stomach until her throat almost closed with it, but she swallowed and glared at Kenneth.

"How *dare* you!" she cried. "How *could* you? In front of *everybody*!"

Kenneth gave her a bewildered look. "But I was only protecting you." His lips pressed together in a hard white line as he turned to look at where Lieutenant Pargeter had escaped into the shrubbery. "Pargeter! He isn't worthy to touch the hem of your skirt—and he was dam—dashed well trying to touch more than that!"

"He was not!" Aimee declared. "I was perfectly capable of handling the situation myself without having you snatch me up like some—some barbarian!" Her conscience pricked her: she had not been precisely sure at the time how to handle Lieutenant Pargeter. But whatever she would have come up with would not have been as embarrassing as being snatched up like a bundle of laundry and thrown upon a horse.

Kenneth's eyes narrowed. "Oh? And what, may I ask, were you doing with him in the first place?"

"What I should have been doing with *you*—walking in Hyde Park—had you come to see me as you had promised!"

She felt his arm stiffen around her, then relax. "You are right, of course," he said, and sighed. A look of deep fatigue came into his eyes. "I am sorry. Sometimes I don't know—I feel—" He shook his head and smiled down at her. "Well, I promise I'll do better, Aimee. I swear it. You will forgive me, won't you?"

Aimee closed her eyes, feeling his arm—strong and warm—around her, how her leg pressed so closely to his. It was the closest she had been to him since his return. She opened her eyes and gazed at him for a long moment. There were shadows under his eyes, and creases at the corners, where there had not been before he left for the army. His skin was brown from the Spanish sun—but how had she not noticed the pallor beneath it? Gently she touched his face. "Are you well, Kenneth?"

"Of course I am!" he said heartily. "Why shouldn't I be? I'm home and have no injuries—much better than . . . half the men in my company." For a moment his smile faded, but his lips turned up again. It was a strained smile, and Aimee had noticed the hesitation before he had answered her.

"I don't believe you, Kenneth," she said quietly.

Almost, she thought she saw fear in his eyes, but he shook his head impatiently. "I don't see why you don't. Have I ever lied to you?" His voice was rough and full of indignation.

"No, of course not. But—"

"Well, there you are. I am quite well." He looked about

him. "Since we are here, and since I daresay you are quite uncomfortable the way you are sitting, perhaps we should walk about a bit."

The wall had come up again. She had put a name to the feeling at last to the distance she had felt before between them, for all of Kenneth's adoring words when he first came home. It was a wall she did not know how to scale or climb or knock down. He had changed, was not the same Kenneth.

And yet, when she closed her eyes and felt his body so close around her, it was so familiar and sure. She did not think she could feel the same with any other man, though she had never been this close to anyone else. An image of Lieutenant Pargeter came to her, and she thought how he looked somewhat alike to Kenneth. Would she feel the same about someone like him, because he looked the same? She was, suddenly, not sure. She did not want to marry a man just because she liked his arms around her. Surely there was more to life and marriage than that.

Aimee gazed at Kenneth and saw him look at her with a slightly anxious expression. She smiled. "Yes, please let us walk. But no more dashing about and hauling me up upon horses, if you please! Perhaps it is something one does in Spain, but not, I assure you, in London!"

Kenneth grinned widely at her, and he looked suddenly like he did when they first met, carefree, with a laughing glint in his eyes. Her heart beat harder—if only he would look at her like that more often!

"No," he said. "It is not something one does in Spain, except perhaps in battle." He let her down gently from the horse, and then stepped down himself.

"We are not in battle here now, Kenneth," Aimee said.

He smiled and brought her hand to his lips. "But of course we aren't," he replied. He turned and spotted some flowers growing near their feet. "Do you still like prim-roses, Aimee? I remember you did . . . a long time ago."

He said it as if it had been a hundred years past. It has not been that long, cried something in Aimee that ached terribly. But she was not sure of his responses anymore, and so only nodded and said, "Yes," and for the rest of their outing only talked of commonplaces, things that even strangers might have spoken of.

"Aimee . . ." Lady Hathaway said tentatively the next evening. "Is it true what I have heard about Kenneth?"

Aimee glanced up from the dress that had been laid down upon the bed. "What have you heard?" she asked. She cast a look at Psyche, who was already dressed, but her friend shook her head at her. No, of course, Psyche would not tell.

Lady Hathaway frowned. "That he ran you down at Hyde Park and threw you across his saddlebow in a most undignified way."

Aimee looked at Lady Hathaway uncertainly. "Well . . . I was not thrown *across* his saddlebow, to be sure!"

"Oh, heavens!" Her benefactress bit her lip, then gazed at Aimee sternly. "I hope this sort of disreputable behavior is not something you are encouraging in my son?"

"Oh, no, ma'am!" Aimee blushed.

"I thought not." Lady Hathaway groaned. "My son has become an idiot." She sighed impatiently. "How this could be when his father is such a brilliant man—and yes, I would even say a man of genius—I do not know. Although, I suppose a superior intellect does not mean one has a particle of common sense about proper behavior. Why only look at Lord Byron, after all! I suppose I should be glad that *my* husband never acted so!"

A giggle erupted from Psyche sitting behind Lady

Hathaway, and Aimee was hard pressed not to laugh, too, and was glad that the maid had pulled her dress over her head at that moment so that her wide smile did not show. The image of the studious and absentminded Sir John Hathaway, graying and bespectacled, as a dark and dangerous poet of magnetic mien—well!

Lady Hathaway eyed her daughter and her friend indulgently. "Really, my dears! It is not as if Sir John could *not* act in that manner. Indeed, there were quite a few times he rescued me from quite uncomfortable situations, before we were married," she said, then frowned. "Even though his wig did have a lamentable tendency to fall off when he did so."

Psyche suddenly buried her face in the pillow upon Aimee's bed, and Aimee swallowed down her laugh so quickly that she choked and began to cough. Muffled shrieks of laughter came from the pillow, while Lady Hathaway pounded Aimee's back to relieve her of her cough.

"Heavens, it is not as if there was *no* dash in your father, after all, Psyche!" Lady Hathaway protested.

"Of course not, Mama," Psyche said, having emerged from the pillow. Her face was a bright pink and her voice trembled with suppressed giggles. Aimee tried not to look at her, for she was certain she would begin to laugh if she did—and really, they shouldn't be laughing. It was quite disrespectful to Sir John.

"However, it is just as well your father does not do such things as toss me across saddlebows—how uncomfortable that must be to be sure!" She turned to Aimee, clearly curious. "*Was* it uncomfortable, Aimee? I imagine one could become quite bruised from such treatment, and if you wish for a salve of any sort, I have some excellent ones," she said kindly.

"Oh, it was a little uncomfortable—my breath was

quite taken away! But I am not at all bruised, so shall not need your salves. How kind you are!" Aimee said gratefully.

Lady Hathaway patted her hand. "Not at all! Are you not to be my daughter-in-law?" She gazed at her shrewdly for a moment. "It is too bad I do not have a salve for embarrassment, for I see how it must be for you . . . and I saw how self-conscious you looked when Lady Handley spoke to you earlier today—was that what she quizzed you about?"

A blush heated Aimee's face, and she looked away. "I—I am afraid I did not deal with her questions as I ought."

"I do not blame you," Psyche said. "Lady Handley is odiously inquisitive."

Lady Hathaway gave her daughter a reproving look. "That is not a very becoming thing to say, Psyche, and I hope you do not speak so in company! However, I quite agree—Lady Handley is very inquisitive and you will always find such people wherever you go. I wish you had told me of the incident straightaway, Aimee, for then we could have discussed how you may respond to such impertinence."

"Have I done very badly, ma'am?" Aimee asked tentatively.

Lady Hathaway smiled. "Oh, heavens, no. It is well known that you are a shy, modest young lady, and cannot wish for such attention . . . and so I imagine that is probably what will be spread about."

"I should think being seized and carried off by one's betrothed would be a wonderfully romantic thing," Psyche said. "I should like it of all things." Her brow creased in thought. "Although if one were to be seized by surprise, it might not be very comfortable." She looked curiously at Aimee. "Do you think perhaps if you had known Kenneth would do it, you might have liked it?"

Aimee smiled slightly. "I am afraid you will think me a dull thing, but even if he had told me about it, I think I would have been just as embarrassed and not agreed to it at all."

"How odd!" Psyche said. "I think I should like it whether it were a surprise or not." She smiled dreamily and twisted a lock of her red hair around one finger. "Just like a knight in shining armor."

Lady Hathaway looked at Psyche hopefully. "Is there . . . is there someone *you* have a *tendre* for, my dear?"

Psyche stared at her mother for a moment, then laughed. "Oh, heavens, no, Mama!"

"Ah, well," her mother sighed. "I daresay you are quite young yet, and certainly you may have another Season if you wish to look about you for a while. However . . ." Lady Hathaway stared off into the distance for a moment, while the two young ladies stayed silent. "However, I think there is something in what you say. It will not do for Aimee to be embarrassed by Kenneth's dashing off with her over his saddlebow—"

"But he didn't—"

Lady Hathaway held up a finger. "No, Aimee, it does not matter in what manner he seized you. You must put a good face on it, and I believe Psyche has something in what she says about it being romantic. Should anyone ask you about it, you may blush all you like, but smile and say how very dashing and romantic you think Kenneth is, and how he cannot bear for you to be without him at every moment, and how jealous he can be of your attention."

Lady Hathaway's words struck hard at Aimee, though her word were obviously kindly meant and for her benefit. She was not at all certain that Kenneth wished to be with her every moment, or that he was truly possessive of her company. She did not wish it to be a lie, but she was beginning to think that it was. If he was possessive of her company, why did he not come to see her every day? It was not enough that he swept her away from a potential rival—if she were to stay at home every time he did not come to see her, she would be as cloistered as a nun. How could she help wishing to go on outings? And he had changed. For all his words—and everyone knew that it was not up to a gentleman to cry off from a betrothal—how did she know he truly wanted her to be his wife?

"Aimee?"

She looked up at Lady Hathaway and Psyche's concerned faces. "Yes?"

"Is there anything the matter?" Lady Hathaway asked, and took her hand, patting it gently.

She looked into her hostess's kind eyes, and almost wept. She so wished her parents had not died! She remembered how loving her own mother had been, and how she missed her warm hugs and kind words, her father's affectionate way of flicking his finger under her chin, his jokes and laughter, and how they had always listened to her childhood confidences. It had been a long time since she had confided anything in anyone.

Lady Hathaway put her arm around her and gave her a brief hug. She waved away the maid who had just finished dressing Aimee's hair. "You are to be my daughter-in-law, Aimee, and I am beginning to love you as I do my own daughters. I think you shall be a good influence upon Kenneth. He loves you, I believe, for all his wild ways."

"I am not sure of that," Aimee blurted, then pressed her lips together in an attempt to press back her tears. She felt a hand pat her back, and Psyche smiled at her.

"Oh, he can be such a stupid thing sometimes, but really he is more intelligent than he seems, and he is very kindhearted, you know," Psyche said. "I think all gentlemen act stupidly from time to time."

"Very true." Lady Hathaway nodded. "Although it is not something one says to them—it would put anyone off, to be sure!"

"Hmm," Psyche said, not outright disagreeing with her mother. Lady Hathaway gave her a look, then turned back to Aimee.

"But, what is it that you mean, my dear? How are you not sure of Kenneth?"

"He has changed, ma'am," Aimee said, and paced agitatedly around the room. "I don't know—perhaps it is because he has been away at war. He acts so strangely sometimes! He used to tell me all manner of things—his dreams, his wishes, that he . . . cared for me. But now he only says he adores me, worships me, and tells me nothing else, no, not even of how his day was spent, or if he will come to a ball with me unless I ask."

Lady Hathaway smiled. "I would think that if he says he adores you, that it would be even better than saying he cares for you."

Aimee shook her head. "It is *not* the same! I don't want to be some marble goddess he worships! I want him to— to kiss me!" She blushed furiously and turned away, putting her hands upon her cheeks.

"Ah!" Lady Hathaway's voice was full of warm understanding. "That is different, indeed. How awkward it would be to have to keep oneself dusted and polished every day and to stay so very still! It cannot at all be amusing."

Psyche laughed out loud, and Aimee could not help laughing as well. "Oh, dear ma'am!" Aimee said, hugging Lady Hathaway. "You are so very good to make me laugh."

"There, there, my child. Of course you wish Kenneth to kiss you. It is a very natural thing when one is in love. Why, when I was betrothed to Sir John I wished it very much—and Psyche you need not look so astonished! Just because I am your mother does not mean I have become insensate, for heaven's sake. But there, you have put me out again." She turned back to Aimee, and this time her gaze was admonishing. "I have long thought, my dear, that you are entirely too modest." Aimee opened her mouth to protest, but Lady Hathaway held up her hand. "No, let me speak! There is nothing wrong with looking one's best and trying to attract attention, particularly the attention of one's betrothed. You have dressed in very good taste, and I have nothing to be ashamed in that. However, there is nothing wrong with a bit of dash in one's dress and nothing wrong with showing off one's assets."

"I have tried to be very good; that is why I have tried to dress properly, and my uncle has always approved of my taste," Aimee said, her voice wavering. "I have tried to be everything my parents would want me to be, had they been alive."

"Oh, my poor, dear girl!" cried Lady Hathaway, moved into giving her a comforting hug. "My poor dear!" She dabbed away a tear with a lacy handkerchief. "Is that what you have been doing? They never would have wanted you to deprive yourself of any pleasure, not dresses or kisses, I am sure! Why, I have always heard they loved you dearly, as I love my own children. I know I would never wish my girls anything less than their heart's desire—though within reason, of course!"

Psyche nodded and patted Aimee's hand. "Yes, Mama is the best of mothers, I assure you, and your parents could not wish anything but the best for you! And though Mama did not wish me to have that lovely *soie de nuit* ball gown—"

Lady Hathaway rolled her eyes. "Much too fast, my love! And *not* the right color for your hair—"

Psyche wrinkled her nose at her mother. "—she did let me have the blue silk overdress, you know the one, Aimee," she continued, then grinned mischievously. "And so I win *that* wager you made with me!"

Aimee's eyes widened. She had thought the blue silk dress quite daring, for it had a low décolletage, no frill or ruching to make it as modest as she thought it should be, and the hem was just a bit above the ankles. Psyche had pooh-poohed her notion, and had wagered that Lady Hathaway would indeed let her buy it. She knew she dressed in good taste . . . but perhaps, just perhaps, just a little dowdily?

Lady Hathaway smiled fondly at Psyche. "Well, it was just the right color, and made your eyes look more blue than gray. But you see, Aimee, I am sure your parents would have wished to see you dress in the very best of styles—what loving mother would not? And there is nothing truly wrong with kissing—" A look of consternation came over her face, as if she were remembering something upsetting. "Of course, you cannot go about kissing all and sundry! Not even for an experiment! Heavens! But it is quite all right if it is with one's betrothed, as long as one does not—That is, if one keeps it to kissing only, of course, and if no one sees one do it." She turned abruptly to Psyche. "And since *you* do not have a betrothed, that is not something I should worry about in you, yes?"

Psyche looked at her mother, wide-eyed. "Of course not, Mama. I did say I had no *tendre* for anyone, did I not? I cannot imagine a more unpleasant thing than to kiss someone for whom you did not feel at least affection."

"That's my good girl," Lady Hathaway said, a relieved look on her face. "Cassandra has a great deal of intelligence, but she had no notion—" She stopped abruptly. "Never mind that! I am sure you will be far more sensible and discreet, Psyche."

"Of course, Mama," Psyche said, and looked extremely innocent.

Lady Hathaway gave her a suspicious look, then smiled at Aimee. "Well, then! You are a lovely girl, my dear. I am sure that all you need is to show it off, and Kenneth will be top over tails in love with you all over again. Not that I think he *doesn't* love you, of course! But he has been away for a long time, and I doubt not that the war has changed him." She leaned toward her confidentially. "Modesty is all very well, and I am glad you are such a good girl. But there is such a thing as being too reticent and it does not help at all to hide one's assets."

A tight, nervous feeling settled in Aimee's stomach. She wanted so badly to do well by Lady Hathaway's generosity, and hated to disappoint her. She had thought she was doing as she ought, and of course she was . . . but it seemed there was more to being presented to society than being good. But she thought of Psyche's dress, and the thought of her bosom being half uncovered and her ankles showing made her feel quite uneasy. She had always chosen clothes with such care, and she hated the thought that she might blush with embarrassment the whole time she was at a ball.

"Please . . ." She hesitated. "Please, may I think about it for a little? My uncle had always approved of the way I looked, and I know he always has my welfare at heart."

Lady Hathaway patted her hand. "You may think about it as long as you like. It will take a while to modify your

dresses and buy new ones after all." She smiled in a con-
fidential manner, as if to a lady of her own years. "You
must remember, my dear, that though your uncle is a very
worthy, good man, he cannot know all of the things that
are so essential to a lady's well-being."

Aimee reflected that this was probably true: she certainly often thought that men were quite contrary charac-
ters, and no doubt they often thought the same about
women. She nodded. "I shall try, my lady."

"That's a good girl," Lady Hathaway said approvingly.

"Oh, Aimee, we shall have some fun—I know the best
place to get ribbons and there is a wonderful dress shop
at New Bond Street," Psyche said, bouncing on the bed
as she sat. "Oh, do say we can get a dress made up for
Aimee for Almack's, Mama!"

"Only if Aimee wishes, Psyche, and do stop bouncing
like a hoyden!"

"Yes, Mama."

"Now, then! I see you are dressed for Lady Connington's ball," Lady Hathaway said to Aimee. "And you look
quite well, as I said you would when I advised you to try
the dress."

Lady Hathaway had selected it for her this once—
Aimee had thought it was quite daring at first for the
bodice was more low than she was used to, and she had
protested, but Lady Hathaway had merely smiled and
handed her a pretty gauze yoke that tied down the front
with ribbons to tuck into the bodice. She could not
protest, then, for it was quite modest with the yoke.

"Thank you, ma'am," Aimee said, and smiled. "You
are so good to me."

Lady Hathaway waved a dismissing hand. "Not at all,
not at all! How could you know how to get on if you do
not have someone to guide you?" She beckoned to Psyche. "Come now, my dear, we must go."

Psyche hesitated for a moment. "Do go ahead, Mama, Aimee. I believe I have forgotten my fan in my room. I shall be down directly."

Lady Hathaway nodded. "Do hurry."

Psyche ran as quickly as she could to her room. "Harry!" she called, as soon as she entered. "Did you hear?"

A glow blazed suddenly next to her and she jumped. Harry grinned at her.

"Must you keep doing that? For heaven's sake, Harry," Psyche said indignantly. "I must have bounced enough to satisfy you by this time!"

"Mmmm . . . well . . ."

"Oh, never mind that!" Psyche said, letting out an impatient breath. "Mama is going to make sure that Aimee is dressed to the nines so as to attract Kenneth. We are going to Lady Connington's ball tonight . . . do you think you can persuade Kenneth to go also? He was invited, but said he could not go. But if you persuaded him to go, perhaps we could shoot him tonight instead of at Almack's."

Harry stared at her. "I?"

"Well, I cannot! I must go downstairs as soon as I can. Oh, I know I left my fan here, where is it?" Psyche hunted amongst the bottles and ribbons at her dressing table.

"How do you suppose I should persuade him? He does not even know who I am, and I am not inclined to let him see me."

"You let Cassandra see you a long time ago, so I do not see why you should not now."

"You were in danger then," Harry said. "I had little choice. And besides, I would have to explain who I am and try to convince him, and that could take a tedious amount of time. He might not even believe me—why should he? It's much better to wait until he and Aimee go to Almack's."

Psyche stopped her search for a moment and looked at him. "Well . . . I suppose you are right," she said, wrinkling her nose at him. "And that is another thing—how will you get into Almack's? You have no voucher, and—" A knock sounded on the door. "Yes?" she called.

"Lady Hathaway says to hurry, Miss Psyche," a maid's voice said from the other side of the door.

"Oh, heavens! Do tell her that I shall be down directly," Psyche said. She turned to Harry. "We shall have to discuss your getting into Almack's later."

"Of course," Harry said, and he smiled mischievously.

"Now I am wondering what horrid trick you are thinking of!"

Harry put on a wounded look, and laid his hand over his heart. "I? A horrid trick? I never do horrid tricks."

"Hmph!" Psyche cast a last look at her dressing table and sighed. "Well, I cannot find my fan, and shall have to go without it." She shifted her shawl over her shoulders and opened the door, giving a glance behind her at Harry. But he was already gone. She shrugged and went down the stairs.

But a small breeze seemed to brush one ear, and Harry's voice said: "I shall bring your fan to you, if I find it."

Psyche smiled. "Why, thank you, Harry—Oh, dear! But you are not invited to Lady Connington's ball! How will you be admitted?"

But Harry did not answer, and when her mother called for her, Psyche had no choice but to hurry down to the carriage.

Eros picked up the fan that Psyche had left in her room. It had been easy for him to find, for she had been in a rush looking for it . . . and he had, after all, hidden it. He wanted some excuse to come to Lady Connington's ball so that she would not be surprised if he came . . . though why he should want an excuse he was not sure. He frowned. He was a god, and could go anywhere if he pleased; he needed no excuse, and he disliked subterfuge unless it served in some way his duties as the god of love. But he knew Psyche would be very uneasy and uncomfortable, and though he liked to tease her, he did not wish her to be discomfited. Humans were so very constrained by their rules! But he supposed that if one were to be around humans often, one must follow their rules so as not to cause an uproar. Uproars were seldom conducive to making people fall in love.

Then, too, it was like a game. Eros grinned. He rather liked seeing how much he could get away with and not disturb—too badly—the equilibrium of human society and those within it. He had found it rather entertaining to see how many people he could lead to the edge of scandal, and watch how they frantically tried to pull themselves back. For the most part, they did, and ended up married, for which he was sure Hera, the goddess of marriage, would thank him should he ever decide to visit her.

Twirling Psyche's fan around by its slender ribbon, he wondered if he should do as Psyche asked, to somehow get Kenneth to come to Lady Connington's ball. He much preferred to wait until Almack's to loose his love darts—or rather, have Psyche loose the love darts. He grinned. It would be much more entertaining at Almack's, for it was a bastion of respectability and strict decorum. However, he was fairly certain that Psyche could not hit the side of a barn, much less Kenneth, so perhaps it could not hurt to let her throw a few. He could tell her he decided to let her try at Lady Connington's, and see how it went. For practice, of course.

Well, then, he supposed he could get Kenneth to come to the ball. He twirled the fan upon its ribbon a few more times in a contemplative manner, then grinned again. But of course he could.

He pulled a sheet of foolscap from Psyche's desk and began writing upon it, and after he was done, sanded it and folded it. He still had the ensign's uniform from when he protected Kenneth during the Peninsular war, and could use it to enter headquarters where Captain Hathaway was now working—Eros had followed him, idly curious about the reason why he was not attending the ball with Aimee. Kenneth was writing a proposal he wished to hand over to his superior officer, Lord Hurst, for the relief of impoverished and crippled war veterans. It was a worthy proposal, and Eros was loath to interrupt him at it, especially since Lord Hurst was to speak in Parliament the next day. However, it could not hurt to see if Kenneth was finished with it, and if he was, to see if he would come to the ball.

Eros snapped his fingers, then frowned at the loud ripping sound as the ensign's uniform formed itself around his body. It did not fit very well; it was very tight across the shoulders, and his trousers did not fit around his thighs properly at all. As a result, the jacket had ripped along the back, and his trousers split along the sides and behind. He remembered that he had allowed himself to grow and age along with Psyche—of course it would not fit. How annoying mortal clothes were!

Well, he would have to find something else. He thought of a lieutenant's uniform he had seen in a tailoring shop earlier today that seemed to be about his size. It was easier than creating one of his own, for he was not at all sure he could get the details right. He would summon the uniform, and of course return it in good condition. He closed his eyes and *saw* the uniform in his mind, then snapped his fingers again and the blue coat and white trousers of the Queen's Own Light Dragoons appeared upon him. He rather thought the braids on it looked quite well on him, and he had always fancied a Hussar's uniform since he first saw one. Then, too, it was a different regiment from Kenneth's, and that of the ensign's uniform he had just tried on, so there would be less chance that Kenneth would remember him. Or so he hoped.

It took only a minute to appear at the door of the barracks in which Kenneth worked. Eros hesitated. Would the note be enough? Perhaps he should look first. Carefully, he drew invisibility around him, opened the door as quietly as he could, and went in.

Ah, perfect. Aimee's portrait was out upon the desk at which Kenneth worked, and he glanced at it from time to time while he wrote. Finally, he put down his pen, reading the words he'd just finished writing. Eros knocked at the door.

"Come!" called Kenneth, without looking up.

Eros opened, then closed the door again, dropping the invisibility around him as he did so. He snapped his heels together and saluted smartly. "Sir!"

Kenneth turned around. Psyche would be concerned if she could see her brother now, Eros thought. The man had shadows beneath his eyes, his hair was mussed, and he looked very tired. Perhaps it would be better if Kenneth did not go to Lady Connington's ball. On the other hand, perhaps a party would be just the thing, a change of venue. It was not good for the man to work so hard; play would be a refreshing change, certainly.

"Yes, what is it, Lieutenant?"

"A message, sir."

Kenneth groaned. "No messages, I'm too tir—" He sighed, then gazed at Eros with a keen eye. "Have I seen you before? Weren't you an ensign?"

Eros suppressed a grimace. Captain Hathaway had a very good memory. "No, sir," he replied.

"Hmm. I could have sworn I've seen you before. What's your name, Lieutenant?"

"Harry . . . D'Amant, sir."

"French?"

"Not French, sir. My family's been around for thou— hundreds of years."

Kenneth grunted. "Old family, then. Well, never mind." He held out his hand for the note. "Here, give it to me." He frowned as he read it. "Who told you to send this?"

"A lady, sir," Eros said. That was the truth, certainly.

"What did she look like?"

"It was hard to say in the dark, sir. I think her hair was red."

"My sister, Psyche, no doubt, although the handwriting looks only somewhat similar to hers. I suppose she was in a hurry?"

"Yes, sir."

Kenneth ran his fingers through his hair. "Devil take it. Well, the proposal's finished and I can make sure it gets into Colonel Lord Hurst's hands first thing tomorrow morning." He sighed. "I'd much rather not go."

Eros hesitated. He was half inclined not to push matters . . . and there was Almack's they'd go to later. But if Kenneth did not come, it was all too possible for Aimee to grow out of love with him, for both had changed in the years they'd been apart. Psyche did not like him to shoot arrows into those close to her, and though she had agreed that perhaps it was necessary during the war to do it to Kenneth, she would not like it if he shot arrows at Aimee. He watched as the captain gazed lovingly at Aimee's portrait. A compromise, then: Kenneth would go to Lady

Connington's ball, but Eros would leave the darts for Almack's.

"She mentioned that Lieutenant Pargeter would be there," Eros said.

Kenneth jerked as if he'd been hit, and he turned swiftly around to glare at Eros. "Pargeter? Damn him! I thought I'd scared him off." A grim look came over his face. "That he dare touch my angel—" He stood up abruptly and seized his officer's coat that he had set aside on the back of a chair. "Get me my horse, Lieutenant."

"Yes, sir!" Eros said, and left the room quickly. He saw a servant and gave him his orders, then left for Lady Connington's ball at her house on a large property just outside of London. It would take only a few minutes for Kenneth to reach the house, for the barracks were not that far from it. Meanwhile, he would return with Psyche's fan, and let her know if he could that her brother would arrive soon.

# Chapter 5

A million candles must have been lit in Lady Conning-ton's ballroom, thought Aimee, for it was exceed-ingly bright after coming in from the night's darkness outside. The light made the ladies' jewels sparkle and showed off their dresses—in all the latest styles—to great effect. It made her suddenly wonder if she was dressed just a little dowdily—not dowdy, precisely, but not at the very height of fashion. She glanced from time to time at the other ladies' dresses and noticed for the first time that their bodices were much lower cut than hers, and cer-tainly more daring. It was not something she had thought much about in the past—she had thought propriety in a pretty dress good enough for her. Even Psyche's dress had a lower décolletage . . . but then, did not Lady Jersey just the other day approve of Aimee's modesty in taste? *Very* modest, Lady Jersey had said.

Aimee sighed, then put on a bright smile as she sat on a chair to the side of the ballroom. Psyche was dancing and chatting merrily with a young Hussar; she was rarely without a partner, for Psyche danced beautifully. Aimee knew she was not as good, but she was very competent nevertheless . . . and yet, here she was, having sat through more than two dances, while most everyone else had been dancing fairly continuously. Perhaps she was not asked to dance much because it was well known Kenneth had returned and that they were betrothed, and perhaps few wished to dance with a betrothed lady.

Aimee looked down at her hands in her lap and bit her lip. That was nonsense, of course. Married ladies were dancing even now, and there was Mary Bramleigh newly engaged to Lord Tramwell, and dancing with any number of gentlemen, including her betrothed.

Well, that was the problem, was it not? Kenneth had not promised he would be at this ball, but he'd sent a note to her and to Lady Connington saying he would try if he could. It was now an hour into the dancing, and he still had not appeared. People could not help noticing his absence; she'd encountered more than a few pitying glances from other ladies who had seen and admired the handsome Captain Hathaway in the past, and she had seen more than a few curious looks from gentlemen.

Perhaps . . . perhaps she was not as attractive as she had thought. She had never really thought of her looks much; she had supposed she looked pleasant enough. It had been four years since she and Kenneth had been betrothed—one could change quite a bit in those years. Perhaps what had been attractive at sixteen was no longer so at twenty. She looked down at her dress again—*very* modest, Lady Jersey had said—and though her light blue round gown was in good taste, one could not say it was precisely dashing. It was, actually, quite ordinary, and perhaps out of step for someone who was betrothed to a man as dashing as Kenneth.

"May I have this dance?"

It was not Kenneth, but Bertie Garthwaite, and she suppressed her feeling of disappointment. Though he was only her cousin, she smiled, and hastily accepted. Bertie was an energetic dancer, and so she did not talk much, but listened with half an ear to his chatter. It was either talking or eating when it came to Bertie—the only time he was silent was at dinner or some other meal. But he was well-known amongst the *ton* and though he was not handsome, he was amiable-looking in a horse-ish way. He was well-accepted as a pleasant fellow, especially if one had a well-laden table, and he gave good advice on what delicacies one should have at one's supper party or ball. He was, in fact, fairly fashionable.

"Bertie," Aimee said abruptly, interrupting a description of a repast he had sampled the day before. Bertie ceased his talk and gazed at her attentively. "Bertie, am I a dowd?"

The music ended, and as he led her from the dance floor, he looked her up and down and frowned slightly. "Mmm . . . not a dowd. . . ."

"But not fashionable either," Aimee replied when he hesitated.

"Well . . . wouldn't say that, precisely. Rather in-between."

"Ordinary, then."

Bertie's mouth pursed in a frowning sort of way, as if he had bitten into a piece of meat and was trying to decide if it was up to his gourmand's standards. He glanced at her face and patted her hand kindly. "Above ordinary, I'd say."

"*Above* ordinary," Aimee repeated flatly. "I thank you."

An alarmed look came over Bertie's face. "Not that you aren't an attractive sort, of course! Very! Just not totally à la mode."

"Oh."

"That is," Bertie said hastily, "no need to be! You're engaged to be married, after all, so that's all right and tight."

Aimee looked up at his face and saw he was clearly anxious not to offend. She smiled and allowed herself to be consoled, and when Bertie offered to bring her some lemonade, she thanked him gratefully and watched him go toward the refreshment table. But she could not help glancing at one lady after another, noticing how the color of a certain dress enhanced the color of one lady's eyes and how the cut of a bodice emphasized another lady's long neck. She gazed down at her dress again—it was pretty enough, but did it enhance any of her physical assets? If she had any, that is? The gauze yoke she wore was very pretty, but few other ladies wore such, unless they were much older matrons.

She noticed how the more dashing ladies—those who wore their dresses cut closer to their bodies, wore bright colors, those who showed a little more bosom or shoulder—seemed to claim more than a passing glance from the gentlemen. Aimee recalled how Lady Hathaway had urged a very lovely dress upon her at the dressmaker's shop, but how she had felt suddenly shy at how revealing it was, and a bit overwhelmed at Lady Hathaway's generosity, and had chosen another, more modest and less expensive dress. The clock struck the hour, and brought her attention to the present. She looked around the ballroom, did not see Kenneth, and wished suddenly she had chosen the dress that Lady Hathaway had presented to her. Perhaps . . . perhaps if she had chosen dresses like that, he would be here now.

"May I have this dance?"

Aimee turned to look—it was not Bertie this time—and for a moment her heart gave a little leap, for the gentleman looked like Kenneth in coloring and height. But he wore the blue regimental uniform of the Hussars, instead of the red of Kenneth's heavy cavalry. It was Lieutenant Francis Pargeter-Hathaway again. Or rather, Francis *Pargeter*. The Hathaways did not seem to like him adding their name to his, though he was related. She hesitated, feeling wary after his behavior such a short while ago.

He smiled ruefully at her. "I must apologize—I know now I should not have acted as I did. I am afraid I was carried away by the force of my sentiments. I will do my best not to act so again."

Aimee blushed and looked down at her hands clasped on her lap. "I . . . I was very surprised, sir, and you cannot blame me for being alarmed."

"No, I cannot blame you, ma'am," Pargeter said forthrightly, and his voice had a penitent undertone. "I have hoped, since I first saw you—"

"Please, say no more!" Aimee said urgently.

A sigh made her look up at him, and there was that mournful look about his mouth again. "I am sorry," he said gently. "I have blundered once more." He bowed, as if to leave.

"No, wait," Aimee said involuntarily. She felt like a perfect wretch. He had promised not to act so again, and he had only done so because he apparently cared for her. He only asked for a dance, nothing more. How could she refuse him that little request? "I will dance with you, this once."

She caught Lady Hathaway's slightly frowning glance, but the lady had turned to Psyche directly afterward and Aimee felt a little rebellious. If Kenneth was not here, at least she could enjoy herself and pretend, just a little, that Mr. Pargeter-Hathaway was Kenneth. They were not truly alike, really, for the lieutenant was not as careless with his clothes as Kenneth, and their manner different, but they were enough so physically that she could pretend. Then, too, she noticed a scratch on Pargeter's face, and thinking perhaps it was from plunging into the shrubbery, felt a little sorry for him. Sometimes Kenneth could be rather alarming, and though she was used to it now, it took a little time for most people to realize there was much kindness behind Kenneth's occasional fierceness. She nodded and rose from her chair.

It was, alas, a waltz.

Aimee wished very much that she had paid attention to what dance might be coming up, but she had been so caught up in thoughts that she had not. If she had, she would have preferred to sit out the dance instead. She had been approved to dance the waltz the last time she had been at Almack's, but she could not like doing it with anyone but Kenneth.

But Kenneth is not here, is he? said a rebellious little voice within her. Lieutenant Pargeter was a fine dancer, more elegant than most. Could it hurt to enjoy herself a little? And why should she not? If Kenneth could not come—and he did not promise that he would—then she should not be pining for him, but put the best face upon her situation as she could. Did not Lady Hathaway say she should make the best of whatever came her way? A tiny doubt niggled at her . . . but Kenneth's note did say that she was to enjoy herself even if he did not come to the ball. And so she would! If anyone else should ask her to dance—the waltz or anything else—she would gladly stand up with them and try her best to put Kenneth's absence from her mind.

She smiled up at Lieutenant Pargeter and if her smile was heavy with determination, her dance partner did not seem to mind, for his hand moved just a little lower from her back to her waist. Aimee immediately began to feel some misgiving. She would be sure to go immediately to Lady Hathaway after this dance, and perhaps Lieutenant Pargeter would feel constrained from asking her for another dance. But it was just one dance, and it would end soon. She had nothing to worry about, of course.

\* \* \*

Psyche wished that Kenneth was at the ball now, though knowing his stubbornness, she was sure that it would take some time for Harry to convince him to come. Though Aimee had not danced more than once with anyone—Francis Pargeter included—she was not asked much, and every time Aimee sat down, there was Pargeter speaking to her. If it were not so well-known that Aimee was betrothed it would seem that Pargeter was trying to steal a march upon Kenneth. Even so, some people still looked upon the pair with raised eyebrows.

She and her mother were doing their best with Aimee, and had already talked about the situation between her and Kenneth. But it seemed from the uncomfortable look that flitted across Aimee's face from time to time, that the poor dear wished her time was not so taken up by Lieutenant Pargeter. Psyche frowned. Perhaps she could manage to get Pargeter away from her friend and so give another gentleman a chance to approach her. She moved toward her friend, and then smiled at the lieutenant, extending her hand toward him and curtseying.

"I was watching you during the waltz—both of you dance so delightfully!" Psyche said. The lieutenant smiled and bowed over her hand, holding it just a shade too long before Psyche pulled away. My, he was an encroaching man! No wonder Aimee felt so uncomfortable.

Aimee shook her head. "Oh, no, Psyche, you know I am not nearly as good as you."

"I cannot agree with you, Aimee," Psyche said. "Although I must say a good dance partner, as I am sure the lieutenant must be, must always show one off to the best advantage." She made herself smile a bit wistfully at Lieutenant Pargeter, knowing full well that she was being quite bold in implying that he should dance with her.

"You flatter me, ma'am," the lieutenant said instantly.

"I have noticed how exquisitely you dance—perhaps you could deign to enhance my poor steps?"

"How kind of you to ask, sir!" Psyche responded, and let him take her hand. She glanced at Aimee, and saw relief flash across her face.

It was a country dance, one that would end up with the beginning pair together at the end. That was just as well, Psyche thought, for she thought perhaps she ought to have a word with Pargeter about staying away from Aimee. Perhaps he was not aware of Kenneth's temper . . . although he should be by now, after the way Kenneth had carried Aimee off on his saddlebow. On the other hand, since Kenneth had carried Aimee off and had not dealt with Pargeter, perhaps he was not aware of Kenneth's hotheaded nature. While she had no affection for Pargeter, she certainly would not want anything horrid to happen to him. He could not be blamed for forming an infatuation for Aimee. She was a very pretty young lady, after all, and a good-natured sort.

But as the dance went on, Psyche could not help beginning to feel uncomfortable around Mr. Pargeter. He had a way of looking at one from time to time as if he were speculating about something—what, she did not know. But she did not like the feeling of being weighed and measured. She was quite relieved when the dance ended; the sooner she would warn him away from Aimee and be done with it, the better.

Psyche waved her hand in front of her face, for the dance had been vigorous, and she wished that Harry had already come to the ball with her fan. Mr. Pargeter gazed at her for a moment, then took her hand and bowed over it.

"I see you have become quite warm," he said. "Perhaps you would like to walk out on the balcony for a little? The night air is not too chill, I believe."

Psyche hesitated. The large ballroom led out to two balconies on either side of the room, below which was a wide moat that Lord and Lady Connington had dug to the Gothic theme of their house. She did not like moats for the most part, for when the weather grew warm they tended to exude noxious odors. However, it was still spring, and the air was cool enough not to bring up any smells. She gazed at Mr. Pargeter again, and hesitated once more, for she thought she glimpsed another speculative expression on his face.

On the other hand, it would be a good place to tell him to stay away from Aimee. Psyche nodded, and let him lead her out the windowed doors to the balcony.

He did not, however, let go her hand once they stepped out into the night air, and Psyche had to tug her hand away. "Really, sir, you should not hold onto my hand so long! It is a most annoying habit, and cannot endear you to any lady."

Mr. Pargeter smiled slightly. "I did not think you would mind, actually."

"I do not see how you can say that. Anyone must be annoyed if they are forced to pull and tug to be released. Indeed, I think your attentions are a bit too pressing—and that brings me to what I wish to say to you, sir!" Psyche eyed him sternly, and was quite put out when he only relaxed and leaned against the balcony wall. She put her hands on her hips. "You must know that Miss Aimee Mattingly is betrothed to my brother Kenneth, and that if your attentions have been as pressing as I have experienced it, it is no wonder that she looks so uncomfortable! I would appreciate it if you did not keep her attention so much and let other gentlemen have their chance at dancing with her."

"I think perhaps it would be up to Miss Mattingly to

tell me if my attentions are unpleasant," he replied, and his smile grew just a little smug.

"Well, I think she did just that the other day when you drove her to Hyde Park. And yet you keep talking to her, and that could hardly encourage other gentlemen to approach her."

The lieutenant shrugged. "If she did not like it, then she should have told me."

"I daresay she did, but you could not take the hint," Psyche retorted. "Haven't I told you that I did not like my hand to be held so long—and you assumed I wouldn't mind! Heavens, that's a piece of arrogance. How do you know it's not the same for Miss Mattingly?" An angry look flashed over Pargeter's face, and Psyche felt a little guilty. Perhaps she shouldn't rake him over the coals so thoroughly . . . perhaps he did not realize how his actions came across to anyone. "I am sorry . . . it just occurred to me that perhaps you might not realize how your actions may appear to anyone else. That does happen from time to time, I know," she said kindly, then frowned a little, contemplating the matter. "Although I have heard that you have very good address—and how puzzling that is! How can one have good address when he does not know how to comport himself?"

"I assure you, ma'am, that I know how to comport myself very well," Mr. Pargeter said, gritting his teeth.

Psyche shook her head contemplatively. "No . . . no, I think you must be mistaken, for just a while ago, you held my hand much too long—twice, in fact! And when you danced the waltz with Aimee, your hand wandered quite a way down from her back to her waist, and I saw she felt quite uneasy. I have not been out about town for long, to be sure, but even I know a gentleman ought not to do such things."

The lieutenant looked at Miss Psyche Hathaway and

felt decidedly irritated. Here he had thought she was willing to flirt with him, or more, but instead she was lectur-
ing him on proper behavior. It was bad enough that he
was only second in line for the Hathaway baronetcy—
which estate had grown quite large in the last few years—
and that he could not borrow on the expectations now that
the war was over. He had managed to do that a few times
when it seemed that Captain Hathaway had been
wounded and fallen ill with fever. But the captain and his
father were now in good health, and he could do so no
longer.

He could overlook that, for he had won quite a bit of
money at the gaming tables lately. But he could not help
wishing to put a spoke in the captain's wheel where he
could. It had angered him that Hathaway had been pro-
moted to captain when he, Pargeter, had not. The man had
got the promotion for actions that were as dangerous as
they were foolhardy, and Pargeter's more sensible actions
were entirely overlooked. Could he be blamed for wishing Hathaway would get his comeuppance?

He had not felt very happy being forced to dive into the
shrubbery at Hyde Park when Captain Hathaway had
nearly run him down. The more he thought of it, and the
more he listened to Miss Hathaway's lecture, the more
demeaned he felt. Anger flared as he gazed at the girl and
he seized her by her arm.

"There, see?" Psyche said triumphantly. "A gentleman
would not seize a lady in such a way." He brought her
closer to him and held her chin in his hand. For one moment a frightened look passed over Miss Hathaway's
face, and he was glad of it. And then suddenly her expression of fear disappeared, and anger replaced it. "If
you are thinking of kissing me because you are angry,"
she said, "or even if you are not angry—you should think
again."

"What, will you scream?" he sneered. "It will only tear your reputation into shreds, Miss Hathaway. And whether it would be saved or no, would depend entirely on me. Think about it."

Her reputation would indeed be in shreds, Psyche thought, and she might have to marry him if so . . . and she should have thought of this before coming out to the balcony with him. But she had assumed he was enamored of Aimee, not her, and so the thought that he might kiss her did not even occur to her. Gentlemen generally did not care to kiss ladies with red hair, for everyone knew that black or blond hair was much more fashionable, or so she had assumed. But it was clear now that they might if they were angry, though why this should be so, she did not know. Well, if he wished to do something disagreeable, so be it. She could be just as disagreeable, for Harry had taught her a trick or two.

Psyche put on a thoughtful expression. "I suppose you are quite right. Well, if you must, you must. Do pray allow me to ready myself." She straightened her shoulders and stepped closer.

Pargeter stared at her, clearly startled at this change of attitude, involuntarily released her chin.

"Well," she said. "Are you not going to kiss me?"

A slow, odiously sly grin formed on his lips, and Psyche gritted her teeth. Wait, she told herself. Just wait. Pargeter took her by her shoulders and brought his lips down to hers. Immediately she lifted her knee sharply into him, as hard as she could, and he doubled over, groaning loudly.

"Oh, dear," Psyche said, making her voice sweetly innocent, "Whatever did I do. I am soooo sorry, Lieutenant! I do not know what came over me and—oh, heavens!" She burst into giggles. "Your clothes!"

A cold night breeze made Pargeter gasp, and he opened

his eyes, tears of pain blurring his sight for one moment before they cleared. He looked down at himself. His legs . . . they had nothing on them. No stockings, no trousers. He closed his eyes again, willing away the pain and illusion that accompanied it. The pain receded, and then the breeze chilled his skin into goose bumps. He opened his eyes. Still no trousers. And his uniform—his blue lieutenant's Hussar uniform. It was gone. He wore, in fact, nothing.

He closed his eyes again, a tendril of dread creeping into his gut. He was, of course, dreaming. One did not wear an army uniform one minute and nothing the next. Or perhaps he was mad. Unless somehow he had lost his memory. Perhaps that was it. He had lost his memory. Somehow he had come out here in the chill spring night and had lost his clothes and did not remember how it had come about.

"Lieutenant Pargeter, I do not think it is at all the thing to be out here without any clothes."

That was Miss Hathaway's voice. He opened his eyes and peered at her. "You . . . I seem to remember you were here a while ago."

Miss Hathaway eyed him curiously. "Yes. I have been here all the while."

"You wouldn't know what happened to my clothes, would you?" he asked, still bent over and frantically trying to cover himself.

"I?" Miss Hathaway said, her hand pressed over her heart. "Why should I know what happened to them? One moment you were beginning to maul me about, and then you are without any clothes. I must say, I never thought one could rid one's self of one's clothes so quickly. How did you do it?"

He stared at her balefully. "You bitch, whatever you did with them, I want them back! I just got them new from the tailor's shop today, and if you've damaged them, I'll have your head!"

Psyche shook her head. "Really, Lieutenant, there is no need to be nasty about it. I do not have your clothes at all, and you may look about you to see this is true. How could I take your clothes away? Did I lay a hand on you? No, I did not! It was quite the opposite! And if you are now here without clothes—a very embarrassing thing, to be sure!—it is all you deserve, for you have been very unpleasant to me, and in fact I think you have been trying to get Miss Mattingly into trouble, which is not at all a gentlemanly thing to do."

"I want my clothes back, damn you!"

Psyche put her hands over her ears. "Such language! No, I am beginning to think you are not at all a gentleman. A gentleman does not use such language around a lady, and he certainly does not shed his clothes the moment a lady appears anywhere around him."

"I did not *shed* my clothes!" Pargeter snarled, and almost rose and stepped toward her before remembering his vulnerable state. He shrank down again, and crawled into a dark corner of the balcony.

"Well, how can I believe that when here you are, without one stitch of clothing on?" Psyche said reasonably. She cocked her head to one side and frowned. "To think that people have been telling me you are one of the dandy set. But here you are without any clothes at all. That does not sound very dandified to me. I wonder, do you do this sort of thing only occasionally, with certain ladies, or is it with any lady at all?"

"I d-don't d-do it at all!" he cried frantically between chattering teeth.

"You know, telling falsehoods does not become you, Mr. Pargeter." Psyche shook her head. "How can you say you do not do such a thing when here you are, obviously doing it? No, though I am not as well-read as my sister Cassandra, I can discern very clearly what is before me!"

Pargeter groaned and closed his eyes. "I am mad," he said. "I have gone mad."

"No, no!" Psyche said kindly. "I think you merely have to rid yourself of this habit of discarding your clothes in front of all and sundry. Especially at balls and other social events."

"I don't—"

"Now, now, Mr. Pargeter! No more falsehoods! That is another bad habit I think you have developed."

Lieutenant Pargeter gave it up—he was becoming numb with cold, and this chit of a girl barely out of the schoolroom had somehow taken his clothes and instead of giving them back, she lectured him on propriety. It did not make sense. Perhaps he was going mad. He wished he had not come to this ball. In fact, he wished he were far, far away, preferably a place with clothes and a warm fire. However, if he was mad, it could be he was not here at all, but indeed at home with a glass of port warming his insides. In fact, he could just be in a drunken stupor, and wake up the next day with a headache, but dressed and blessedly warm.

A stiff, freezing wind blew upon his bare backside and demolished this hopeful flight of fancy. He curled himself into a miserable ball in his corner of the balcony and began to rock himself to and fro.

"Are you well, Mr. Pargeter?"

"No," he mumbled. "Go away."

"How rude!" Psyche said. "How you came to have a reputation for good address, I do not know!"

"Psyche!"

Lieutenant Pargeter's body tensed. He recognized that voice. It was Captain Hathaway's. A thought pushed itself through his tortured brain: Miss Hathaway was the captain's sister. Suddenly the unearthly image came to him of Hathaway's face the day the captain had bore down upon him and Miss Mattingly in Hyde Park like a demon from the nether realms.

"Oh, dear. I do believe my brother is here," said Miss Hathaway. "I do not think he would like to see you in this state, Mr. Pargeter. You are not properly in uniform, after all."

Pargeter made a low, desperate moan and searched frantically about him for another exit than the ballroom, but there was none.

"You could always go over the balcony," Miss Hathaway said helpfully. "There is a moat down below, full of water to cushion your fall, and it is not all that far down. You will be quite safe, I am sure."

Lieutenant Pargeter peeked between the stone balusters of the balcony. He did not like heights, but the image of an enraged Captain Hathaway came to him again. Quickly he scrambled up from his hiding place and vaulted over the balcony.

"Psyche!"

Psyche turned to her brother, and smiled. "Kenneth! I thought perhaps you were not coming to the ball." Her brother stormed onto the balcony, his eyes narrowed with suspicion and anger.

"Pargeter! Where is he?"

A splash sounded below them.

"Pargeter?" Psyche asked. "As you see, he is not here."

Kenneth looked at his sister suspiciously. "I was told he had come out here with you."

Psyche shrugged. "Well, he certainly is not here now." She brightened. "But never mind that. How happy I am to see you! You have been working much too hard lately."

"Well of course I am here, especially after that message you sent me." Kenneth continued looking suspiciously about the balcony.

"Message?"

"Yes, Lieutenant Harry D'Amant gave it to me."

"Harry D'Am—Oh! Yes, of course, Harry."

Kenneth turned a distrustful eye upon his sister. "You know this fellow well?"

"Oh—well, yes, on and off through the years. He came to visit our neighbor when I was a little girl long ago, and I have seen him from time to time while you were away." Psyche felt a little anxious; she had never really discussed Harry with anyone, and except for Cassandra who did at last see him some years ago, everyone believed him to be her childhood imaginary playmate. She seldom spoke of him now, except to Cassandra from time to time. "A childhood friend. Surely you must have heard me speak of him?" She tucked her hand in the crook of his arm, and they walked from the balcony into the ballroom.

"Hmm. No, I have not, not that I can remember." He grinned suddenly. "A beau, Psyche?"

Psyche blushed. "Oh, heavens, you know I do not have beaux! Why, my hair is the wrong color." The thought of Harry as one of her beaux—ridiculous, of course. He had been her friend too long for that. Besides, she had never heard of anyone having a beau with wings. It would be an awkward situation to explain, certainly. "No, really, Kenneth, he is just a friend."

Kenneth looked at her in a critical manner. "Well, you have grown up into quite a lady, dear sister, and believe me, red hair has nothing to do with whether one has beaux or not."

"Really, Kenneth?" Psyche smiled at him. "I hope you are right."

"In fact, I do believe Bertie would be interested—"

"Only because he thinks my hair resembles a goulash

of carrots," Psyche retorted. "That is not the way in which I should want a beau to think of me."

Kenneth laughed, then sobered. "Well, whatever beaux you decide to acquire, I hope you stay away from Francis Pargeter. I don't trust him."

Psyche nodded. "I do not think he is quite the thing. In fact, I think he is trying to get Aimee into trouble with you."

"The bast—deuce take him! As if she could ever—Which reminds me! Where is he?" Kenneth's brow darkened.

Psyche giggled. "I think he is probably swimming in the moat."

"The moat? That's a dashed strange thing to do at a ball—you're not hoaxing me, are you?"

"No, I am not! Really, it is all your fault for almost running him down in Hyde Park, and for looking so odiously fierce just now when you came out to the balcony. He saw you coming toward us and decided the best thing to do was jump over the balcony into the moat."

Kenneth gave his sister a long look. "And why did he decide that?"

Psyche widened her eyes innocently. "Because I suggested it to him, of course."

"I think there's more than you're telling me." He looked at her suspiciously.

"Oh heavens, Kenneth, do leave it alone!" Psyche said, letting out an impatient sigh. "The reason I wished you to be here was because I thought it better if you attended Aimee rather than . . . anyone else."

"Pargeter, you mean."

"Well, yes. It's been a long time since you and Aimee have really been together, and sometimes I wonder if two people can change so much that they don't know each other well anymore. If that's the case, then doesn't it stand to reason that you and Aimee should get to know each other all over again?"

Kenneth stiffened. "I have not changed."

"I think you have." Psyche looked at him and thought she saw a flicker of fear in his eyes . . . but what had he to fear? "But whatever you think, there is Aimee now—do go to her! Would I be much mistaken if I assumed you went right past her in your pursuit of Lieutenant Pargeter?"

"I . . . I suppose I did."

"Well, then! I suggest you go to her now."

"Well, I—"

"Captain Hathaway, sir!"

Kenneth turned. "Oh, is it you, D'Amant?"

Psyche swallowed her gasp and coughed violently instead. Oh, heavens, it was Harry! He was wearing a blue Hussar's uniform, and looked quite handsome in it. Psyche wrinkled her brow: the uniform looked oddly familiar.

"Yes, sir!" replied Harry, and gazed at Kenneth respectfully. He turned and smiled at Psyche. "Miss Hathaway dropped her fan, and I thought perhaps I should bring it to her."

Kenneth cast a sly glance at Psyche. "Very good of you, Lieutenant," he said. He bent toward Psyche and whispered in her ear, "definitely a beau!"

Heat crept into Psyche's cheeks, and she slapped her brother's arm. "Don't be an idiot," she hissed. "He is only a friend!"

"Of course," Kenneth replied, grinning. "If you don't mind, D'Amant, will you take my sister off my hands for a few minutes? I need to see to my betrothed."

Harry gave an elegant bow. "My pleasure, sir." He took Psyche's hand and led her away.

Kenneth nodded and looked about him. There! Aimee

was sitting by herself, looking quite lost. The quick disorientation that usually went through him whenever he gazed at his betrothed caught him, and he put his hand over the pocket where he usually kept her portrait—but it was gone. A sudden panic seized him—he must go back and get it. But Aimee had looked up and seen him, and her face lighted with a smile. No, it was foolish to go back to the barracks for the portrait, for he was here now at the ball, and it would seem very odd for him to leave again so soon. He stepped forward and took Aimee's hand in his and lifted it to his lips.

"Well, it seems I was able to come, anyway," he said. "Is my mother here?"

"She is, but once she saw you introducing Psyche to that handsome young lieutenant, she felt comfortable enough to retire to the card rooms," Aimee said. "I am so glad you did decide to come after all!" A concerned and guilty look came over her face. "Although . . . now you are here, I almost wish you had not."

Pargeter, Kenneth thought angrily. He's stolen a march on me. "If you did not want to see me, Aimee, I wish you had told me earlier."

Aimee frowned. "Of course I wished to see you! It is just that you look very tired, and now I feel like a horrid selfish creature for wanting you here for something as frivolous as a ball, when you should really be resting."

"Well, it's too late now," Kenneth snapped, and regretted his words, for Aimee paled and glanced away.

"I am sorry," he said immediately, but there still must have been an edge to his voice, for Aimee looked at him, her lips pressed firmly together, and a spark of anger in her eyes. An irritation grew in him, and a sudden odd wish to see her portrait again—he did not have to worry about her reactions when he looked at the picture, and he did not have to think of so many things at once, only gaze at it and think of how perfect she was.

But this woman before him—she was not perfect. Yet, she was Aimee, his betrothed, the woman in the portrait. For one moment he closed his eyes, feeling dizzy with fatigue and confusion, then stared at her again. Of course she did not change to what he thought she should be. Nothing had been what he thought it should be when he had returned to England.

"Kenneth?" Aimee said tentatively. "Are you truly well?"

"Yes—!" He barely bit off the curse that came to his lips. Why did everyone keep asking if he were well? He looked about him and saw some of the guests glance at him curiously. "I think we should dance," he said. "It is what we are here for, after all."

He thought she would refuse him, for his voice came out more curt than he intended, and she hesitated. He almost apologized for it, but she spoke before he did.

"Yes," she said, and held out her hand so that he could take her to the dance floor.

They were silent—he did not know what to say after such an uncomfortable start. But he felt sorry for speaking so sharply; she had meant well, he supposed, and at the very least he could try to be pleasant.

"Do you like London, Aimee?" He asked, as he twirled her around the ballroom to the beat of the waltz. He felt awkward talking to her, as if she were less his betrothed and more someone of recent acquaintance.

"It is very amusing," she replied. "I miss home sometimes, though."

"Do you think . . . do you think perhaps we might go there for a while?"

Aimee looked warily at him, then smiled tentatively. "I would like it of all things, but I would not like to disappoint Lady Hathaway and cut short the schedule she has laid out for me."

"Is—is it Pargeter, Aimee?" he asked in a rush. He did not know quite why he asked it, and let out an impatient breath at himself. "He came to call upon you, and then you went to Hyde Park—"

"I do not know why you should be concerned whether I see him or not—just because I am betrothed to you does not mean I should be cloistered like a nun." Aimee's words came harshly from her before she could stop them, and then a sudden rebelliousness and weeping despair choked her throat and kept her from taking them back. Did he not love her anymore? Was this his way of giving her an opening to break their betrothal? She should, of course, for she could not bear the thought that he'd marry her out of honor and not out of love.

He had loved her once—she was sure of it. She gazed at him, clearly seeing how the war had changed him, how it had sculpted his face to leanness and put shadows under his eyes. She could not make him look like the youth she had known, but perhaps she could make him love her again. But how was she to do this? She knew very little of how a woman lured a man to desire her. But she thought of what Lady Hathaway and Bertie had said about her clothes and her style, and how the gentlemen at the ball had looked at women more stylishly dressed than she.

Then, too, Kenneth had not seemed to like her to be with Lieutenant Pargeter; it was the only time he felt moved to be with her, so that he could take her away from his cousin. Perhaps there was some little bit of love for her left in him, and perhaps it made him jealous when she was with another man. She gazed at him, and saw his lips pressed together tightly when she mentioned Pargeter— yes, that must be it.

"If . . . if I go on an outing with Mr. Pargeter—or any other man—when you do not wish to, what is wrong with that?" She nearly stumbled over her words, and she did not like to provoke him, but if it would cause him to come to care for her more, then she would. She swallowed down her fear and lifted her chin in defiance. She supposed another woman would demand to break the betrothal, but she could not do that; she had lost people she loved before, and she could not bear to have it happen again. Aimee gazed at him, and saw a dangerous light in his eyes. She shivered a little, knowing what it was, for though he had never directed that look at her, she had seen it directed at others, and trouble had definitely resulted. So be it, she thought. If it would bring him back to her, so be it. The music was ending, and he slowed his steps, bringing Aimee to the side of the room.

"I believe we should walk about a little," he said abruptly. "There is something we should discuss."

"As you please." Aimee said. Perhaps if they went somewhere private, they could talk of the problem between them . . . although she was not altogether sure of this. The dangerous look was still in Kenneth's eyes, and she did not quite know how he would act toward her. Perhaps it would be best if she put on a nonchalant air. "It is crowded in here, and hot. I daresay it would be better to go elsewhere." She waved to the windowed doors that led to the balconies. "Lady Connington has opened the doors downstairs to the garden—she has put Chinese lanterns all along the rows, and I have been longing to look at them."

Kenneth stared at her for a moment. "Your wish is my command," he said, and there was a sharp, ironic note in his voice.

Aimee let out a long breath. Perhaps in his anger he would be forced to say what he felt. Then, at last she would know what to do. Quickly she pulled on her shawl that she had left on a chair, and Kenneth took her hand and they left the ballroom.

The night was clear and cool, and Aimee had been careful to choose a thick woolen shawl to put about her. She should not have shivered so, but she did, and knew it was because she feared a little what might come of their "discussion."

The gardens behind the house were lighted by the candlelight that shined down from the ballroom above, and the imported Chinese lanterns hung on rope tied to poles set along the path between the flower beds and shrubberies. Lord Connington had returned not long ago from China on a diplomatic mission and had brought back many of the lanterns. They were made of paper and lacquered wood, some round and some box shaped, but all of them elaborately decorated. They swung gently in the breeze, and gentle tinkling floated in the air from the bells that hung suspended from beneath the lanterns. It was not as bright here as it was in the ballroom, and Aimee almost regretted suggesting they come out here; she could not see Kenneth's face or expression as clearly as she could indoors.

And yet, his steps suddenly slowed, and the tension seemed to leave him—she could feel it in the hand that clasped hers. Perhaps . . . perhaps his anger was gone. Aimee allowed herself to relax. She glanced at him again—his face was in shadow, as was hers, she was sure, despite the lanterns. She did not know what to say to him, but she felt she must say something. One brightly colored lantern caught her eye.

"Oh, look at that one!" Aimee exclaimed. She pointed to one with a bright red dragon. "Isn't he magnificent?"

Kenneth nodded, then looked at the other lanterns. "There are twelve different animals on each one, I see . . . and I think they represent the months of the year. If I am not mistaken, the Chinese have a different astrology than ours, and each month is represented by an animal." He looked at her assessingly. "I think perhaps you must have been born under the sign of the rabbit."

"A rabbit! I suppose it is because I am a timid thing that cannot even say boo to a goose. That is not very flattering, to be sure!"

"Or a cat," he said. She could see his mouth move in a grin, and her heart lifted. She laughed.

"Oh, now I am cattish! No thank you!" She looked him over in return. "And I think perhaps you must have been born under the sign of . . . oh, perhaps the horse. No, perhaps the ox. You are certainly as stubborn as one."

"What, not the dragon?"

"No, a dragon might be dangerous—I would not like to be sacrificed to one, you know." She gave him a smiling, mischievous look.

Her lips curled up just at the corners when she smiled and he remembered how he thought when he first returned home that she was full of curls and curves. For some reason, he had not been enthralled by it—perhaps it had been because he'd been so blasted tired. But now . . . now the night sculpted her face into something more oval, and made the bright curls of her hair look soft. She looked very much like the portrait. He gazed at her eyes; they were shadowed with the dark and seemed inviting, and her mouth looked sweet with untasted kisses.

He brought his hands up and cupped her face between them, and her smile faded as she stared at him. He looked at her lips, parted now, her breath coming a little faster between them, and slowly, slowly he closed his eyes and kissed her.

Memories of softness and curving flesh pressed

against him so very long ago rose in his mind and mixed with the image in the portrait, and then became real, no dream, for Aimee's arms came around his neck and she moved against him, moving her mouth upon his. He pulled her closer against him, deepening the kiss.

And then, suddenly, there were voices near. Startled, he parted from her.

"I forgot," he said. "I should not have done that—we could have been seen."

Aimee smiled and touched his face tenderly. "I do not mind it, we are betrothed after all, and—oh, Kenneth! It has been so long!"

So long . . . it seemed an age ago, and when he looked at her lips and the long line of her throat, the tired emptiness in him that seemed so ever present these days cried out to be filled. He looked about the garden and saw a less lighted path where a tall weeping willow tree grew. He took her hand and led her to it.

"Aimee," he whispered, and pulled her into the shadows of leaves and branches that hung down to the ground. He bent and kissed her again, pulling at the ribbons of the gauze yoke that covered the base of her neck. He closed his eyes and felt the remembered softness of her lips, the smoothness of her skin. It confused him—he could not see her in the dark beneath the tree's branches, only the cool remote face in the portrait, but his hands and lips remembered and yearned for something his eyes could not. He kissed her upon the flesh just under her chin, and she drew in a sharp breath, as she had long ago before he'd gone to war, when he first kissed her there. She put her hands on either side of his face and drew him up and kissed him fiercely. This he remembered also, and laughed softly, for she had always done this, changed from soft kittenish brushes of her hands to a rush of passion and sleek feline movements in one fiery instant. It

had aroused him then, as it did now, and with it came relief. This was the way they should be, as he remembered,
with none of the awkward distance he felt with her since
his return. With a sigh he moved his lips to her throat and
shoulder.

Aimee moved against him, kissing him wildly. She
could not stop herself now, for she felt as if she had been
a starving woman given her first taste of food. It had been
so long, and every sight of him since he returned made
her yearn more for him, for he had not touched her until
now.

"Ah, Aimee, sweet," he murmured, and kissed her
neck again. She felt his fingers at her throat, and suddenly
the gauze yoke around her neck fell away. Instinctivley
she put her hand up to cover herself, but he pulled her
hand away. "Let me kiss you, love. It's been so long." His
lips came down again upon hers, and then moved to her
cheek, below her ear, and slowly, slowly slipped down to
her throat. She felt his hand move to her bodice and push
aside the gauze still tucked into it. He sighed, and ran his
fingers above and between her breasts, then kissed the
trail his fingers made across her skin. He moved her back
and she felt the edge of a bench against her legs. His
hands ran behind her, and gently he picked her up and
laid her down again.

His hands moved upon her in ways she remembered
and in ways she had forgotten or had never known. The
hot kisses upon her mouth she remembered, but not the
hard urgency of them. She remembered his hands caress-
ing and shaping her breasts, but not without the screen of
silk or muslin between flesh and flesh. This was Kenneth
whom she knew and did not know, and it was like loving
a stranger to whom she felt she belonged, heart and soul.

"Ah, God, Aimee, how I want you." His breath came

from him in a groaning sigh. "But not here, not here." He pulled her up to sit upon his lap, kissing her all the while.

There were voices again, closer, and Aimee moved reluctantly away from him. She looked up at him, but could not see him in the darkness, at least, not well. Touching his cheek, she murmured, "I love you, Kenneth."

Once more he pulled her to him and kissed her deeply. "Sweet, dear Aimee. I need to see you again soon, alone."

Love rose hard and quickly within her; it was like a deep ache in her heart. "Yes," she said, seeing only shadows upon him in the dark; she touched his face, letting her fingers see for her. "Soon." He kissed her once more.

"Yes, soon," he repeated, and awkwardly tucked the gauze yoke into her bodice again. His fingers touched her breasts, and she drew in a sharp breath.

"If . . . if we are to stop now, I think I should do that," she said shakily.

He kissed her ear and whispered, "Next time, leave it off," then drew her shawl around her shoulders before leading her back to the Conningtons' ballroom.

Aimee drew in a joyful, happy breath. So she had been right. He did care for her, and it was jealousy that finally brought it out at last. And if she dressed more in fashion, no doubt he would care more. Well, if that was what it took, then she would do it again until he finally treated her as he had before he had left for the war.

When they came into the light of the ballroom, Aimee caught him looking at her, puzzled, as if he had suddenly encountered a stranger. It made her uneasy . . . but it did not matter, she told herself. She knew what she needed to do, and she would do it.

Psyche watched her brother walk toward Aimee and saw the smile of relief and welcome light Aimee's face when she spotted him. "Well, that's all right, then," Psyche said, turning to Harry. "How did you manage to gain an invitation? Lady Connington is very particular about whom she invites."

Harry lifted his eyebrows haughtily. "I am a god. It matters not who Lady Connington invites; I go where I please." His expression suddenly changed and he grinned mischievously. "Actually, I merely begged entrance so as to return Aimee's portrait to Kenneth—which I picked up from his desk. I think he would be better off without it, though, don't you think? The less he looks at it, the less influenced by it he will be."

Psyche looked at him admiringly. "Oh, that was very clever of you!" She felt curious, however. "You must have done more than that," she said. "She could have just had a servant take it from you and give it to Kenneth."

"No, she could not have. I also told her I must return your fan to you, for I would die a thousand deaths before I would let a common servant convey such a treasure to Miss Psyche Hathaway." His grin grew wider. "Lady Connington is a terrible romantic, I have discovered."

"You didn't!" Psyche pressed her hands to her cheeks in a vain attempt to suppress her blushes. "Now she will think you are my beau, when you are only my friend."

Harry looked at her thoughtfully. "Does that bother you, then?"

"Yes—no! Oh, heavens, I don't know!" Psyche said, frowning. "I only know that I am used to—more comfortable—thinking of you as my friend."

He patted her hand comfortingly. "Never mind it, Psyche. I hope you will continue being my friend; and it could not hurt pretending I am your beau, could it? Practice, so to speak, until you have a real one."

Psyche thought this over. It would be a pleasant thing to have beaux, as other young ladies did, and not have to sit out any dances—and she so did like dancing! She nodded. "Very well. I daresay it will be fun—and oh, that means I will not have to wait upon Kenneth to escort me about here and there, will I?" She smiled widely up at Harry. "Well, even better! I am very glad you suggested it. Only . . . do you dance? I don't think I have ever seen you do it."

Harry smiled. "But of course I dance." He took her hand. "Shall I show you?"

She looked toward the dance floor—another waltz was being set up. "Yes, please," she said and curtsied. The music began as they came to the line of dancers, and Harry swept her into it. She smiled at him. She should have known he would be a fine dancer, for he had always moved gracefully; she felt as if she were floating above the floor, and looked down just in case he might have made them do just that.

"You don't trust me," Harry said, and his mouth turned down in exaggerated sadness.

"But of course I don't," Psyche replied. "You are wont to play tricks."

"Not on you, surely."

"No . . . I suppose not. Not lately." Psyche admitted. She glanced at him, then looked at him up and down. "You look very fine, indeed! Although . . . the uniform looks very familiar. Where did it come from?"

Harry shrugged. "I saw it in a shop earlier today and fancied it. I had an ensign's uniform from some years ago when I was watching over your brother, but it did not fit anymore. However, I thought the lieutenant's uniform would do, and so I summoned it."

Lieutenant . . . tailor's shop. "Oh, heavens," Psyche breathed. No, it was not possible. . . . "Harry," she said tentatively, then bit her lower lip before continuing. "Harry, when you summon things, do you summon them from where you saw them last or where they happen to be at the time?"

"Well, since one cannot be sure an object will be where one saw it last, naturally I summon it from wherever it happens to be."

"And . . . and if it happens to be on a person, would it suddenly disappear from him?"

Harry grinned widely. "It has been known to happen from time to time."

"Oh, dear, oh, dear!" she gasped. "I thought it might have been you, but you weren't here, and so I could not think—oh, heavens!" The laughter that she had kept repressed upon the balcony when Lieutenant Pargeter lost his clothes swelled and she burst into giggles. "Oh, you should have seen Pargeter! One m-moment he was trying to k-kiss me and then the next moment he compacted himself into a ball and tried to wedge himself into a corner of the balcony!"

Harry's grasp tightened. "Did he hurt you?"

Psyche gazed at him wide-eyed. There was a slight frown between his brows. "Oh, no," she said. "I am afraid I hurt *him*. I—I, well, I am afraid I struck him in a vulnerable spot, as you taught me long ago, but he did make me quite angry with him."

"Hmm."

"Oh, really, Harry, you needn't worry. I told him he might want to jump over the balcony into the moat and he was quite obliging about it, so I imagine he isn't as bad as I first thought him."

A gleam entered Harry's eye. "He jumped into the moat?"

"Yes, although I think perhaps I might have been a little mistaken saying it was not that far down. He did jump, anyway."

Harry grinned. "*Very* obliging of him," he said. "I suppose I need not do anything to him—for now."

"No, certainly not!" Psyche said. "Besides, he is probably somewhere else in the house now. Although . . ." Her voice wavered. "Although I wonder how he is going to gain admittance to the house again without any clothes on? I cannot imagine Lady Connington will admit a naked man into her house." Her shoulders shook and she burst into laughter. "Oh, dear! Harry, we must stop dancing, or else I shall fall from laughing so hard, I swear I shall."

Harry swept her away from the dance floor and led her out past the windowed doors to the balcony.

"Oh, no—a balcony!" A vision of Lieutenant Pargeter's horrified face and scrambling limbs as he vaulted over the low wall into the moat seized her mind's eye and Psyche began to shriek with laughter. She pressed her hand against her mouth and snorted instead. "Oh! Oh, dear! Oh, Harry, I cannot stay here, for I swear I shall die laughing. And if Mama came to hear how I am acting so uncontrollably, I shan't hear the end of it—But heavens, the way he looked when he scrambled over—!"

"I wish I had seen it," Harry said, and began to laugh as well. "Do you suppose he is still swimming about in the moat?"

"Ohhhh!" wailed Psyche, "you are making me laugh even worse, and I am sure people are wondering what is going on."

"Psyche! Are you out there?" came Lady Hathaway's voice from just inside the ballroom.

"Oh, dear, it is Mama!"

"Quickly, put your arms about me," Harry ordered.

She obeyed without thinking, and her breath was almost taken away when her feet left the stone floor of the balcony and she found herself high in the night sky. "Harry, what are you doing?"

"Protecting your reputation," he said. He flew up past the window of the upper floor, and Psyche dared gaze down.

At last she felt something solid beneath her feet. She stood up gingerly and opened her eyes. "Where are we?"

Harry grinned. "On the roof."

"Oh, dear."

She could see the light from the ballroom shining down upon the gardens below, and the hanging Chinese lanterns swinging gently, looking like fireflies from so far away. "How pretty!" she exclaimed. "I am glad you brought me up here . . . although, I think that even if Mama had found us together on the balcony—" Psyche laughed.

"No," Harry replied. "I have been in your world enough to know that if she had seen us together, she would have got *ideas*."

"It is hardly *my* fault that you acted as if you were in love with me in front of Lady Connington and in front of Kenneth!"

Harry clasped his hands behind him and tipped back his head and gazed at the moon. Psyche watched how the moonlight played over his face, outlining every perfect feature against the night, and it seemed almost for a still moment that he could have been a marble statue. Then he sighed and moved, and the illusion was gone. "Well, I wished for a legitimate reason to be invited to stay at the Conningtons' ball," he said. "You would hardly wish me to cause a stir by appearing out of nowhere in the middle of the guests, would you?"

She smiled at him. "It was rather clever of you to think of such an excuse, actually."

"I think your mother will ask about me anyway . . . and

I did say I would pretend to be your beau—just for fun, you know. I expect that Kenneth will be squiring Aimee about more often now, so I thought . . . I thought perhaps you might not mind it if I went about with you, not invisible, you see." There was a wistful note in his voice, and it occurred to Psyche that perhaps being invisible except to only one person might make him feel rather lonely. Her heart melted, and she put her arm around him in a brief hug.

"Of course I do not mind! Are you not my dear friend? I think it will be great fun to introduce you to my family now—well, perhaps not as the imaginary friend I used to speak of! But perhaps I can say that I have known you for a long time, perhaps when . . . oh, I know! You came many years ago, when we were children. Perhaps you are our neighbor's—Sir William Hambly's—distant relative. I do not think he has any, actually, and he is so old now that I understand he does not remember people much anymore. So it would be very understandable if you ever met and he did not remember you." Psyche bit her lip in thought. "I do not like to lie, of course. But I don't know how else to explain you, for I don't think Mama would believe me if I told her who you actually are."

"Perhaps not," Harry said. "Or, I could prove it to her, but I think it would be a bit of a shock if I did. Best to do this sort of thing gradually."

"Of course."

An uneasy silence came between them. Another change, thought Psyche. He is going to be visible to everyone now—a good change, though, for she could not wish her friend to be lonely. A chill breeze blew upon her and she shivered.

"You are cold," Harry said instantly, and took off his coat and put it around her shoulders. He held out his hand. "Come, I think we should return, and perhaps look

at the picture gallery or some such, just to show that we
have been very proper."

She put her arms around his neck again, and he held
her around her waist as they slowly drifted down to a spot
in the gardens.

They went up the steps to the ballroom, and when they
entered it, Harry bowed and kissed her hand and took his
leave as if he were any other gentleman who had been invited to the ball. It was just as well that he left, for as soon
as he did, Lady Hathaway bore down upon Psyche, curiosity clearly on her face.

"Who was that young man, Psyche?" she asked. "I
must say he was quite attentive toward you, and quite as-
tonishingly handsome!"

"Oh . . . oh, that was Mr. Harry—Henry—D'Amant. I
have known him forever," Psyche said.

"French?" Lady Hathaway asked.

"Oh, no! His family has been around for thou—that is,
hundreds of years. As long ago as the Norman Conquest,
at least."

"Well, an old family, then." Her mother cast her a suspicious glance. "How is it that you have known him forever, and I have not?"

Psyche hesitated. She did not want to tell a lie, but she
knew she would not be believed if she told the truth. But
perhaps she could tell mostly the truth, and it would not
be so bad. "Remember, Mama, my friend Harry—you
know, my invisible one?"

Lady Hathaway smiled. "Of course I do! You had such
an imagination, child!"

"Well, he was real in a sense. He was really Harry
D'Amant. We met when I became lost in the woods at
home, and he brought me back. He's a distant relative of
Sir William Hambly, our neighbor, and was visiting
then."

"Sir William? But I thought he had no relatives."

"Mr. D'Amant is his only one, I believe, and very distant," Psyche said. She sighed. Lying should not be so easy, but it was and very convenient, too. "I remembered him because he helped me when I was so afraid and . . . and made up my imaginary friend from him."

Lady Hathaway laughed. "Well, your imagination did elaborate quite a bit upon him! Wings and a white dress, I remember you said!" She paused and stared at Psyche in a speculative way. "I must say, however, that such an angelic description would fit him perfectly—I have never seen so handsome a young man. And Sir William's only relative . . ." A slow smile grew on her face.

"Mama!" Psyche said indignantly, for it was clear that her mother had concluded what Psyche had overlooked entirely: that since Harry was supposedly Sir William's only relative, he must obviously be his heir, and Sir William owned a great deal of well-tended property. "Mama, it is not what you think! Harry is only a friend, I assure you!"

"Of course, my dear," Lady Hathaway said, and patted her daughter on her shoulder. "No doubt we shall be seeing more of Mr. D'Amant?"

Psyche rolled her eyes. "I hope not, if you are thinking perhaps he might have a *tendre* for me, for he does not."

"I am sure you are quite right, love," Lady Hathaway said, and smiled smugly.

"Mama!"

"Tut, tut, Psyche! I am sure it is nothing, as you say. But it is getting quite late—Kenneth has already taken Aimee home—and we must go now. I wish you to get plenty of sleep, for nothing can be more off-putting than dark circles under one's eyes when receiving callers."

*"Mama!"*

But Lady Hathaway merely smiled again and bade her

give Lady Connington a good evening so they could leave and then began to talk of Kenneth and Aimee—she was beginning to think they were becoming more comfortable with each other. Finally, they entered the coach, then rode down the road back to London. Psyche relaxed against the squabs and thought over the evening and chuckled quietly. She supposed it would be vastly more entertaining with Harry going to balls with her and—oh, dear! Psyche sat up with a jerk.

"Is there something the matter, my dear?" her mother asked.

"Oh, no . . . nothing. I thought I had forgotten something, but I see I have it in my reticule after all."

"Thank goodness for that!" her mother replied.

They had forgotten something—Psyche had intended that she and Harry try to shoot Kenneth with love darts here instead of at Almack's but they hadn't done anything of the kind! And to think that they had every opportunity, too. Psyche sighed. She supposed too many things had happened for them to remember.

Perhaps it would be enough if Kenneth no longer had Aimee's portrait. He had spent a great deal of time with Aimee this evening from what her mother had been saying. Well, the next day would show them what to do, she was sure.

# Chapter 6

"Where is it? Damn, I know I had it here last night!" Captain Hathaway turned over the papers he had scattered across the desk in the barracks. Nothing. He looked at the mess he had made in the room he had worked in the evening before. Papers slipped off books and he had accidentally tipped over an inkwell. He had lost the portrait of Aimee.

He sat down abruptly in a chair and pressed his hands to his eyes. Where had he put it? He remembered setting it down on the desk and gazing at it from time to time while he wrote, but he did not have it in his pocket when he had come to Lady Connington's ball. He closed his eyes and groaned. He had to have the portrait. He'd be lost without it.

No, of course he would not be lost but . . . he did not want to be without it. It was what had sustained him during battle, had given him heart enough to go on. A hard, hot feeling pressed upon his chest, suspiciously like grief, and he let out a harsh breath. Nonsense, it was only a portrait. One did not grieve over a portrait.

Did he drop it, perhaps, on his way to Lady Connington's ball? He had certainly been in a hurry. But, no, he did not remember putting it in his pocket. He thought of who might have taken it—it might be anyone. Who had been in the room that night? No one, really. Well, there

was Lieutenant D'Amant, but why would he take
Aimee's portrait, when he was clearly attracted to Psyche? It made no sense. Kenneth sat down on a chair and
sighed wearily. Perhaps he could find D'Amant and ask
if he had seen the portrait anywhere.

He stood up quickly and began to pull on his jacket. A
wave of dizziness struck him and his sight dimmed, making him sit down abruptly. He closed his eyes and took in
a deep breath, trying to slow his racing heart. Tiredness
overcame him, and for one long moment he wished desperately to lay down where he was and sleep forever. He
shook his head slowly. There was no reason for him to
wish to sleep—he slept too much lately as it was.

No, he had too many things to do and needed to find
the portrait. He would do that first, then sleep.

"Mr. Henry D'Amant," Trimble announced, as he opened
the door of the Hathaways' drawing room. Lady Hathaway threw Psyche a triumphant glance, which her
daughter studiously ignored. Lady Hathaway let out an
exasperated breath. Why had she such stubborn and contrary daughters she did not know. First there had been
Cassandra putting off her suitors with her blunt blue-
stocking ways, and now Psyche was proving difficult. A
great many gentlemen had shown an interest in her, but
she had shown no preference for any of them.

But as she gazed at Mr. D'Amant, hope rose in her
heart. For how could any young lady be proof against
such a man, even her stubborn daughter? He was tall and
well-built, especially across the shoulders if the perfect
fit of his Bath superfine coat was any indication, and as-
tonishingly handsome. She watched with an excusable
smugness as some of her female guests became slack-
jawed and then clearly envious when he went straight to
speak with her daughter. Even Aimee, whom she was

sure was totally in love with Kenneth, gazed upon Mr. D'Amant with a certain awe.

Further, he was possibly the only heir of Sir William Hambly, and though that gentleman was ancient and feeble in both mind and body, there was nothing feeble about his estates or his investments. The disposal of Sir William's estate had been an item of discussion of all his neighbors of late—it was thought a pity that it should go back to the Crown instead of being given to a descendant.

She watched as Mr. D'Amant said something that made Psyche laugh. They would certainly make a handsome couple, and what a coup it would be to have Psyche married off creditably in her first Season!

Her gaze went to Aimee, and she smiled at her fondly. She could not be greedy—she was marrying off Kenneth this year, after all, and that would take up a great deal of her energy also, to be sure. Aimee looked away to address the comment of a lady to the other side of her, and Lady Hathaway allowed herself to frown a little. She was becoming concerned about Aimee—the girl did not confide in anyone, which she could understand. Anyone who had lost one's parents would not be used to revealing her thoughts or feelings to others. But the girl had been looking tired and worried of late, though today she looked much better. Lady Hathaway wondered if London life was too fast-paced for a country miss like Aimee, and if it was fatiguing her. Perhaps it would be better to cut short their stay in town and go home early. Suddenly the door burst open, making Lady Hathaway look up in alarm.

It was Kenneth, looking disheveled and quite wild. He glared around the drawing room before encountering her stern eye and then subsided, straightening his jacket with a sharp jerk before proceeding further into the drawing room. He paused for a moment as he caught sight of Mr. D'Amant, then gave his mother a brief kiss on her cheek.

She patted his hand but held it firm so that he was obliged to stay by her side. An aura of barely subdued restlessness surrounded him, and as she gazed at his face she became worried. Dark shadows were beneath his eyes, as if he had not slept in a month, and his face looked very lean and taut with tension. "What is the matter, Kenneth? You do not look well at all."

"I am quite well, Mother," he replied, his voice terse, almost snappish. He encountered her admonishing gaze and pressed his lips together before he continued, "I am sorry, ma'am. It is just that I have lost something and I wish to find it right away."

"What is it, my dear?"

"Aimee's portrait. I left it in the barracks when I went to Lady Connington's ball, but it is not there."

"Oh, dear," Lady Hathaway said. "Perhaps you mislaid it?"

"No," Kenneth said shortly. "I need to talk to Mr. D'Amant—he was there last night."

Lady Hathaway frowned. "Surely you don't think he stole it?"

"I don't know, but he might have seen it."

She stared at her son, alarmed, for there was a feverish air about him. "Perhaps I should bring him to the library," she said. Kenneth nodded, and abruptly turned and left.

There was something definitely wrong. Kenneth had not even looked at Aimee, much less spoken to her, and the poor girl looked very discomfited at the way the other ladies cast her pitying glances. Surely they could not have fought? Lady Hathaway mentally reviewed her son's entrance into the drawing room, and how Aimee had looked with gladness at him. No, it was not that.

She went to Mr. D'Amant and gave him Kenneth's

message, and was relieved to see the young man receive
it with brows raised in surprise and a nod of acquies-
cence. She felt she was a good judge of character; Mr.
D'Amant, she felt, could not have done anything wrong.
He left, and she sat down again with her guests, and
began to listen with considerable absorption to Hetty
Chatwick's recitation of certain delicious pieces of scandal she had picked up at the last performance of the
opera.

Perhaps it was because she was so absorbed that she
missed entirely Psyche's exit from the room, and when
she looked up again it was too late for her to go after her,
for she could not leave her guests without a hostess. Lady
Hathaway frowned. She would have to speak with that
young lady soon about her deportment. She was getting
entirely too impertinent and neglectful of her duties.

Kenneth's anger and frustration faded when Mr. D'Amant
walked into the room. The man's face was totally devoid
of deceit or guilt; there was polite curiosity on his face
perhaps, but that was all.

"You wished to speak to me, sir?" Mr. D'Amant said
politely.

"I—I, er, yes." Kenneth hesitated. He had come into
the house thinking only that he must retrieve the portrait
from the only person he was aware of who could possibly have taken it, but he had seen the young lieutenant's
clear interest in Psyche in the drawing room, and if the
fine cut of his coat was any indication, Mr. D'Amant had
no need to steal Aimee's portrait for either love or money.
And yet . . . and yet when he had asked for information
regarding Mr. D'Amant's whereabouts, no one at headquarters had any record of him. That, at least, was suspicious.

"I . . . I am looking for something, Mr. D'Amant, and was wondering if you might have seen it last night."

The young man raised his eyebrows in question. Kenneth began to feel embarrassed at the mad impulse that drove him to question someone who seemed, except perhaps for one thing, quite innocent.

"A portrait of my betrothed. I had it in the barracks where I was working when you came in to give me my sister's message, but it is not there."

"And you suspect me of taking it?" Mr. D'Amant pressed his lips together in a thin line, his chin lifted in hauteur, obviously insulted.

Kenneth could feel his face become warm, and was annoyed at himself to be outfaced by a subordinate. "I have not said that," he replied. "I am sorry if I seem to have implied it."

"Then why do you wish to speak to me, sir?"

"I was wondering if you might have seen it."

Mr. D'Amant's expression was still stiff, but he replied, "Yes, sir, I have. It was on your desk when I delivered your sister's message to you. I noted it particularly because it was a very well-done painting."

"Have you seen it since that evening?"

Mr. D'Amant gave him a haughty look. "No, I have not." There was a pause, then he continued. "Is there anything else, sir?"

"Only that there is no Lieutenant Henry D'Amant in the Eighteenth Hussars." There, the last thing that would make his inquiries legitimate—what if D'Amant was a Bonapartist spy?

"May I suggest you check again, sir? I believe General Marston will speak for me. And if you wish to see my papers, I can certainly have them delivered to you." He gazed at him calmly, but there was a clear undercurrent of anger in his voice.

General Marston! The general had been involved with military intelligence. If Mr. D'Amant had worked with him, then certainly his name would not be well-known. Kenneth suddenly felt extremely stupid and foolish and wished desperately he had not been so impetuous as to seek out Psyche's beau and ask him questions that were downright accusatory. If General Marston would vouch for Mr. D'Amant, then there was no question that the man was a lieutenant indeed. If D'Amant wished to call him out, he would certainly be in his rights to do so. He pressed his hands against his eyes and groaned.

"I am sorry, Mr. D'Amant. I don't know what—I have been a fool."

There was only silence as Mr. D'Amant stood stiffly and stared at him.

"If you wish to call me out for insulting you so, then I will certainly meet you."

"No, I think not . . . particularly because I believe Miss Hathaway would have my head on a platter if I hurt you." The young lieutenant suddenly grinned, and Kenneth could not help liking him in that instant.

"What, do you think you'd pink me?" he asked.

"But of course. I'm a tolerable good shot, I believe."

Kenneth grinned at the total assurance in Mr. D'Amant's voice. "I'd like to see that—I've shot the pip out of an ace at fifteen paces, and haven't seen anyone beat that yet."

"Twenty paces," Mr. D'Amant said instantly.

"Damned shame I don't have a playing card at hand to see you do it, Mr. D'Amant."

"Call me Harry," Harry said pleasantly, and pulled out a deck of cards from his coat pocket. He shuffled through the deck and pulled out a card. "An ace of hearts, sir?"

Kenneth laughed. "You're on!" He strode to the mantelpiece and brought down the brace of pistols that hung above it. Carefully he cleaned and loaded them, and handed one to Harry. "They're the finest sort," Kenneth said. "Nicely rifled barrel, hair trigger. Shoots straight every time."

Harry set the playing card on the mantelpiece and measured out twenty paces from it. Taking aim down the barrel, he carefully squeezed the trigger, and a loud report sounded in the room.

Kenneth whistled, examining the card. "Bloody hell. Right in the middle of the pip. I've never seen a shot like that in my life." He turned to Harry. "Got another card? Damned if I won't give it a try, too." Harry flicked him another playing card and Kenneth took up the other pistol after he placed the card on the mantelpiece.

He also measured out twenty paces, but just as he pulled the trigger, the door burst open.

"*Kenneth*! "What in *heaven's* name are you doing?" cried Psyche, her face pale.

"Now look at what you've done," Kenneth said irritably. "You made me miss my shot."

As his sister looked at him and Harry, her face turned furious. "How *dare* you scare me like that? The way you were glaring at Har—Mr. D'Amant in the drawing room, I was sure you would do him some damage. And then the shots—!"

Kenneth turned to Harry and grinned. "Looks like I'm the one to have my head on a platter."

"This is no laughing matter," Lady Hathaway said sternly, stepping into the library. "I am much displeased with you, Kenneth. First you come storming into my drawing room most rudely, and then you ruin the library wall." She turned to Harry and pointedly eyed the pistol in his hand. "And you, young man! I never would have thought you the sort to be so lost to propriety as to encourage him. That is hardly the way a guest should act!"

"But I—"

"I do not want to hear it!" Lady Hathaway said, holding up her hand. Psyche almost began to laugh, for the two men looked suddenly abashed, and she had never seen Harry put so out of countenance. "Heavens, Kenneth! I thought you had outgrown such antics long ago! And I *would* like to know what either of you plan to do to repair the wall!"

"Manton's," Kenneth said apologetically. "Much better to practice there."

"I should think so!" Lady Hathaway said.

"My deepest apologies, my lady," Harry said, and bowed over her hand. "But I daresay the damage is not as bad as you might think." He waved at the wall over the mantelpiece. "Perhaps you would like to inspect it?"

Lady Hathaway walked up to the wall and stared at it. She raised her brows. "Hmm . . . I can hardly see it. How odd. I would have thought it would have made a larger hole than that." She turned to Kenneth. "Well, since you are here, you might as well help me entertain my guests. Heaven knows I tried to get your father down to see to them, but there is no dislodging him from his study once he has his nose in a book of Sophocles or Asch—Asch—whatever it is."

"But I—"

"Hush!" Lady Hathaway commanded, taking his arm. "Come with me, if you please!"

Harry gave Psyche a look and slightly jerked his head away from the door. When her mother and brother left, she closed the door, leaving it slightly ajar for propriety's sake as she had been taught.

"What is it?" she asked, turning to him.

"I think . . . I think it is not enough that the portrait was taken away, Psyche."

"Oh?"

"He accused me of stealing it! Me!" Harry frowned, clearly offended.

"Well, you did steal it."

"No, I only borrowed it. But he would not have accused me in such a way if he were not so enamored with it . . . and if there was not something wrong with him."

"You have seen it, too, Harry?" Psyche said, sitting on a sofa near the window. "I thought at first he was only being stupid and forgetful, but I think it is more than that. It's as if he can't stay still for fear of—of something. He moves about all the time, and is never still."

Harry nodded thoughtfully as he sat next to her. "Yes. It makes him act differently from the way I thought he might."

Psyche looked at him surprised. "That is the second time in the space of a few months that I have heard you admit to a mistake."

"I did *not* say I made a mistake!"

"Ah. I see." Psyche rolled her eyes up at the ceiling.

"I must say you can be infuriating, Psyche!" Harry said, standing abruptly from the sofa. "I have been at shooting my arrows for millennia, and know what I am doing—certainly more than you do."

"Not if you make mistakes—and don't say you haven't, because you have!"

"I rarely make mistakes, and when I do, it's only one or perhaps two at most. I know all I need to know. I am a god, and that is enough."

Psyche eyed him shrewdly. "I don't think that is enough. I have sometimes thought it is too bad that you are not mortal, for then you would know exactly what your arrows do." She looked at the stubborn tilt to his chin and shrugged. "Well, think on it, if you please! You just might learn something." She went to the door and opened it.

"Wait!"

Psyche paused and looked back at him.

"Anyone else would be punished severely for such hubris," he warned. Psyche stuck her tongue out at him. For one moment his brows drew together in a frown, but then he laughed. "Very well! I'll see if I can get Kenneth to change back at Almack's." He sighed. "I suppose I will need to give him back the portrait, so that he can fall out of love with it."

"Why can't you do it here?" Psyche asked.

"It's too small a crowd, and we'd be noticed," Harry replied.

Psyche gazed at him for a long moment, suspicious of his innocent expression. "Well . . . you will give me some darts, too, won't you?"

"Of course," he replied, his voice smoothly bland.

"Are you trying to trick me?"

"No, of course not!" Harry said indignantly.

"Well, you had better not," Psyche warned. "Or I promise I shall not speak to you for a week."

"Oh, please, not that!" he said in tones of abject horror.

"You are odious!" she said, and stomped out of the library.

"Anything you say, Psyche," Harry said sweetly, and followed her out the door.

The drawing room was stuffy, especially since the windows were closed and the sun was streaming through them, making the room even warmer than it was five minutes ago. Kenneth stifled a yawn and managed to smile politely at Lady Greene, an elderly lady who was very shortsighted and very long-winded. She had a habit of peering at him as if trying to discern his expression and moving too close for comfort. More than a few times she had almost spilled her cup of tea into his lap, and all he got for it was an apology and a high-pitched titter. He cast an agonized glance at Aimee, who gave him a sympathetic smile, but was herself cornered by another elderly lady of loquacious habits.

At last the callers began to leave, and it was with a sigh of relief that Kenneth rose from his chair. If this was what he would be forced to do if he practiced shooting pistols within doors, he would be very certain not to do it again. Not that he usually did—for some reason he had not thought of the consequences. It was not something he had to think about much when he was away in Spain; one could easily find a place to practice one's shooting wherever one might be—well, look at Harry D'Amant, after all! He had not hesitated to shoot the playing card, either. Perhaps it was a habit that military men had a difficult time changing. But it was not done that way in London, and he supposed he should become used to it. Ever since he had returned to England, there seemed to be thousands of things to which he needed to become accustomed. He looked out at the bright sky barely discernible between the buildings outside, and felt as if they were closing in on him. A light touch on his sleeve made him turn and rise from his chair.

"Will I see you at Almack's, Kenneth?" Aimee asked.

"I—yes, of course," he said, smiling down at her.

She gazed at him closely. "I wonder now if you should. Perhaps it would be better if you stayed at home and rested. You look very tired, Kenneth."

"Why *is* it that everyone tells me I look tired?" he exclaimed impatiently.

"Perhaps it is because you do look it," Aimee said. "Really, you need not come this time."

"I am well, I tell you!"

Aimee hesitated, then nodded. "As you say, then."

Kenneth gazed at her downturned face, and felt immediately remorseful. He smiled at her a little stiffly. "I am sorry. I had no cause to snap at you, when you were only caring for my welfare. I wonder that you wish to marry me, for all my bad temper," he said.

"Of course I do," Aimee said instantly, an anxious look on her face.

He let out an impatient breath. "There is no need for worry, Aimee. Upon my honor I would never cry off our engagement—I can't, after all."

Aimee gazed steadily at him, her heart dropping to her stomach. "No, you wouldn't want your honor so stained. But if you could, would you?"

He frowned. "Of course not. I keep my word."

"That's not what I meant, Kenneth."

"Well, for heaven's sake say what you mean, then!" he snapped.

Angry heat flushed her cheeks. "You will not speak to me in that manner," she said.

"Oh, Lord," Kenneth said, and sighed, pushing his fingers through his hair. "I'm sorry, Aimee. I—I suppose you're right. I am a little tired. Nothing that a short nap couldn't fix, though." He smiled, but his mouth was strained at the corners. "I will see you later, at Almack's, then?"

Aimee nodded slowly, still staring at him. She needed to speak to Lady Hathaway . . . Kenneth had never acted in this snappish way before, not that she could remember.

"Very good." He patted her on her back. "I'll take you to Hyde Park tomorrow, too."

"No, really, there is no need," Aimee said. "I would much rather you have rest."

He looked at her sharply, and she was sure he bit back a retort, but his face softened. "I'm not much of a husband-to-be, am I? I'll try harder, I promise you, Aimee."

Aimee smiled at him and nodded. But when he left, she

sighed. Perhaps she should tell Lady Hathaway about
Kenneth, that she did not think it was a good thing for
him to accompany them to the routs and parties he had
said he'd attend. It could not hurt to cut short their season—unless Psyche minded, and she was sure she would
not if she was told that Kenneth was not feeling well. Yes,
she would speak to Lady Hathaway about it; her hostess
loved all her children dearly and would not wish to have
any one of them be the slightest bit ill.

Immediately she felt lighter, as if a large stone had
been lifted from her heart. It would be, admittedly, a relief for her also. She liked to be amused and enjoyed the
theater and the balls, of course. But she missed the fields
and the woods and the long rambling walks she and Kenneth used to have out in the countryside. They used to
talk of everything then . . . now it seemed they talked of
nothing at all.

Yes, she would talk to Lady Hathaway, and they could
go home, and everything would be much better, she was
sure.

Aimee sighed and looked at the clock on the mantelpiece; she was the last to leave the drawing room, for
Lady Hathaway had discreetly shooed the guests out so
that Aimee and Kenneth could speak in private. She grimaced. She hoped it was not as clear to everyone else as
it was to Lady Hathaway that all was not right between
her and her betrothed.

Aimee pressed her lips together. Well, she had
promised herself she would make it right, had she not?
She had clearly seen at the Conningtons' ball that she
needed to show off her assets—as Lady Hathaway had
put it—and so she would. Kenneth had even preferred her
dress to be a bit more fashionable than she had allowed it
to be. If that was what she needed to keep her betrothed
by her side, she would do it. She had three dresses that

had come in from the dressmaker's today, and she needed to look at them and decide which one she would wear to Almack's. She would make sure they were more daring and more fashionable than the other dresses she had; she would flirt as best she could, and if that made Kenneth more jealous, then so be it. She closed her eyes, remembering the evening before out in the Conningtons' garden. Yes, if that was what happened if she made sure to dress less modestly and dance with other gentlemen, then it was worth it.

A tremor of uncertainty still made her pause as she opened the door to her room, but she quashed it firmly and went to the wardrobe in which her maid had told her the dresses were hung. She opened it, and searched through her dresses—yes, there was the blue sarcenet with the net overdress. She pulled it out and laid it on her bed.

It would not do. The neckline was far too high; she wanted something daring. Quickly she went through the rest of her dresses, old and new, and just as quickly began to feel a definite depression of her spirits. *All* of them had modest necklines! Had she been, after all, that prudish? Lady Hathaway had not said so in so many words, and neither had anyone else to whom she had spoken—of course they would not! They were too polite to say anything about it, she was sure. She remembered Lady Hathaway urging what Aimee had thought were very daring dresses upon her. She remembered Lady Jersey's comment that she was a *very* modest young lady. Most of all, she remembered all of Kenneth's disappointed and confused looks whenever he gazed upon her. It seemed she was not quite up to anyone's expectations.

A sudden boiling rebellion seethed in Aimee's heart, born partly from resentment that her mode of dress—that *she* was not quite acceptable as she was, and partly from yearning to be, just once, daring and popular, betrothed or not. Quickly, she went to a sewing basket she kept near the wardrobe and pulled out a pair of scissors.

Snip! Off came the long gauze portion of the sleeves from the blue sarcenet. Snip, snip, snip! Off came the better portion of the silk bodice. Aimee gazed at it with savage satisfaction. There! It was as daring as anything she had seen on the members of the *ton*. She was a good needlewoman; all she needed was to hem the sleeves and sew the gauze from the sleeves just under the deep *V* she had made in the bodice. Her needle and thread whipped through the cloth with a sure, swift, angry motion.

At last it was done. Aimee gazed grimly at the blue sarcenet gown. She knew just which corset to wear with the dress, too. She would have her hair dressed high upon her head, and wear only one thin chain upon her neck with a small pearl pendant at the end of it. Lady Hathaway had mentioned showing off her assets. So be it. Nothing would detract from whatever asset she had.

A knock sounded at her door just as Aimee put away her sewing basket and hung up the dress in the wardrobe again. "Come in," she called.

Lady Hathaway entered. "I have just come to remind you to get yourself ready—we are going to Almack's tonight, remember. Have you chosen your dress?"

"Aimee nodded. "Yes, ma'am. The blue sarcenet."

Lady Hathaway frowned for a moment, then nodded reluctantly. "Yeeess . . . I suppose that will do." She sighed. "It is a *very* modest dress, but still in fashion. Certainly it is nothing of which the patronesses could disapprove."

A flicker of guilt made Aimee glad the deepening gloom of twilight dimmed the room enough to hide her blushes. But Lady Hathaway's words—especially the word *modest*—banished most of the guilt she had.

"Not—not as modest as it was, ma'am," she blurted, however. She at least should mention she had changed the dress. "I took the gauze sleeves off, and modified a few other things."

Her hostess glanced at the clock. "Well, I would look at it, but we have not much time, and you are an excellent needlewoman, so I am sure you have done it justice. I will send Gwennie up to you after she is done with Psyche." She smiled and patted Aimee on the cheek. "You need not look worried. Kenneth will be there, after all, and I am sure he will dance with you at least twice." She sighed. "Well, then, I suppose I must go see to Psyche. She has such difficult, wayward hair! I am never sure if it will hold up as it should." She moved to the door, and with one last smile at Aimee, closed it.

Aimee gazed after Lady Hathaway for a moment after she left, then took in a deep breath. Well, that was that. She would wear the dress, and if Lady Hathaway did not like it when she saw it, it would be too late. She pressed her lips together firmly. She did not care. Perhaps everyone thought she was a dull, dowdy nobody. Tonight, she would show them she was not.

Lieutenant Francis Pargeter-Hathaway contemplated his reflection in the mirror as he adjusted his neckcloth. He frowned, then smoothed a slight crease. There. He looked quite fine, if he did say so himself, and nothing could be better than the new waistcoat he had just bought. It had cost a pretty penny, but he had just won a game of faro the night before and was fairly plump in the pocket now. He deplored the kneebreeches that were de rigueur at Almack's, but one did not buck the dictates of the patronesses there, not even gentlemen.

He frowned in the mirror as his valet dressed his hair, and wondered if he should go to Almack's. He had dis-

creetly asked here and there if Captain Hathaway would
be attending, but could find no definitive answer. The
chances were that the captain would not, for he had overheard his family's talk of the man being overworked or
ill, and at one rout he had heard Lady Hathaway saying
that she would excuse her son from attending for some
reason or another.

Not, of course, that he was afraid of the captain. Pargeter had, after all, not done anything that should have
brought Hathaway's ire upon his head. At least, not
openly. He doubted Miss Hathaway had told her brother
about the incident at Lady Connington's ball, for Hathaway had only given him a bland look when they happened to have passed each other at headquarters. No
doubt Miss Hathaway had thought better of revealing
something that could not reflect well on her reputation.
Pargeter felt a little more cheerful at the thought. No, he
had nothing to fear. No doubt Hathaway did not even understand what went on around him, for he was not really
very clever. He'd heard the man say so himself more than
a few times during the war.

Which made it all that much more infuriating that
Hathaway had attained the rank of captain, and that he,
Pargeter, had not. It would have made more sense if it had
been the other way around. He had made more sensible,
less risky choices than Hathaway. How could anyone
have not seen that? It was clear even now how much superior a man he was than the captain; Hathaway was a
man without finesse and fit badly into society. Anyone
could see that.

No doubt Hathaway would have been barred from Almack's, had it not been that he was fortunate enough to
be let in by Lady Cowper, who happened to have formed
a friendship with Hathaway's sister, Lady Blytheland.
Pargeter sighed with impatience. There was another puz-

zle—Lady Blytheland was another who was without finesse and was vulgarly blunt-spoken. It made him quite doubt Lady Cowper's reputation as a shrewd judge of character; clearly her softheartedness was more in evidence in these instances.

Well, he would show them all that Hathaway was not worthy of being there, and that Pargeter was the superior man. And if he could lure the captain's betrothed into thinking so as well, all the better. Not that he had an affection for the chit; she was too dull by half. But it would be quite a coup to lure her out from under Hathaway's nose.

Pargeter inspected himself in the mirror once more and smiled complacently. Yes, he would show them all.

# Chapter 7

By the time the Hathaways' coach came up to Almack's door, Aimee was sure her stomach rumbled from anxiety as loudly as the coach wheels had on the cobblestones. Perhaps she had miscalculated on the depths of the cuts on the bodice when she had altered the dress; she had been, she admitted, just a little angry. She should not have been, for Lady Hathaway had been kind to her and had shown her the right way in which to go about in society. She was grateful to her hostess for it. But Aimee could not help feeling she was lacking; she could see other ladies' assessments of her dresses, how their eyes had quickly gone over her clothes and how they had turned away with a dismissing air, or how there had been just a little bit of self-satisfaction in their gaze. She had not minded it, for she had been fairly sure of Kenneth's affections, and that was all that had mattered to her. Now she was not so sure of him, and Lady Hathaway's and Kenneth's view of her seemed all of a piece with everyone else's apparent assessment.

So when she altered her dress she felt a certain angry defiance. And even when she had put on the dress and saw how it scarcely covered the tips of her breasts and how she seemed to almost overflow the now strap-like blue silk and gauze bodice, she had gazed at herself in angry satisfaction and taken a slight vengeful joy in the maid's scandalized gasp. With her hair piled high atop her head and the thin silver chain around her neck, the upper part of her body seemed almost bare. Her pelisse had covered it up, and neither Lady Hathaway nor Psyche had seen her alterations. And at that time she did not care.

But that was in the safe confines of Lady Hathaway's house. Now she was here at Almack's, where the disapproving eye of Lady Jersey or Mrs. Drummond-Burrell could banish a young lady from society forever. Aimee's mouth felt dry, and she wondered if she could somehow keep her pelisse on inside the ballroom. She almost groaned. She would look more dowdy—in fact, outright peculiar—than if she had not altered her dress at all.

She had her shawl, at least. Though perhaps . . . perhaps she should tell Lady Hathaway. Yes, she should tell her, and perhaps they would go back—it was not necessary that they go to Almack's every week, after all. The coach door opened, and taking in a deep breath, Aimee turned to Lady Hathaway.

"Ma'am, I think I should tell you—"

Lady Hathaway waved her hand at her. "You can tell me later, Aimee. If you do not go out now, we will lose our opportunity to get past this crush—watch your plume, Psyche! You almost bent it on the door frame!"

Aimee climbed out. Perhaps before they entered the ballroom, she would tell Lady Hathaway; surely there would be time to do that there.

But there was not. Almack's entryway was crowded with guests and there was scarcely room to move, much less get Lady Hathaway's attention, for that good lady was already talking to various friends. Psyche had gone forward, her coat already taken away by a servant. A footman waited politely for her pelisse, and Aimee clutched the collar—she could not go in the ballroom in her pelisse!

Hastily she draped her shawl about her and unbuttoned the pelisse, then pulled the shawl around her neck as the footman took the coat. She was, for now, well covered. Where was Lady Hathaway? Oh, dear. She had already gone upstairs and the ballroom door was opening. Aimee swallowed. She could not stay down below. She took another deep breath and quickly ascended the stairs.

"Are you feeling a chill, my dear?" Lady Hathaway asked. She was standing next to a young gentleman who looked at Aimee with slight interest. Aimee ignored him—now was the time to tell Lady Hathaway about the dress.

"No—yes—this dress—"

"Looks very well, Aimee, and I see you have taken off the sleeves. An improvement, I am sure. And here is Lord Varley, my husband's acquaintance." She looked meaningfully at Lord Varley.

Lord Varley looked startled for a moment, then smiled pleasantly. "If you would do me the honor of dancing with me, Miss Mattingly?"

It was clear that Lord Varley had not thought of dancing until Lady Hathaway had prompted him. Aimee felt half inclined to refuse, but caught sight of Lady Hathaway's kind and encouraging face. What was she to do? Aimee put a smile on her face and adjusted the shawl closer to her neck. Perhaps the shawl would stay where it was. She hoped so. "Yes, thank you," she said, and took Lord Varley's hand.

And felt the shawl slipping from around her.

"You do not need this, I am sure," she heard Lady Hathaway say from behind her. Frantically, Aimee tried to hold onto the shawl but she missed it, and suddenly felt Lord Varley's hand tighten on hers. She looked up at him, but he was obviously not looking at her—or rather, not at her face. It seemed his attention was riveted somewhere around the pearl pendant on the end of her necklace.

It was the worst dance of her life. It was, thankfully, a relatively sedate one, with no hops or jumps, and she managed not to stumble or make a false step. But the same could not be said of her partner, or of a few other gentlemen who passed her in the figures of the dance. Her face grew hot and she kept her gaze down upon her feet, for she could not bear to catch sight of Lady Hathaway and the probable expression on her face. She wished desperately the dance would end, that she had not let her temper get the better of her, and that she hadn't changed the dress so drastically. And at Almack's, of all places! How much more stupid could she have been?

At last the dance ended, and she dared look up. Clear astonishment was on Lady Hathaway's face, and Aimee could not bear the disapproval she was certain she would hear from her hostess.

"A dance, Miss—?" It was another gentleman, one she remembered stumbling as he passed her in the last dance. She glanced at Lady Hathaway's now slightly frowning face, and Aimee admitted to cowardice: she looked at the gentleman and nodded her head and once again was swept off into a dance before Lady Hathaway could get to her.

This time the gentleman did not stumble, but he danced too closely for comfort. Perhaps it would be better to face Lady Hathaway—she would have to, sooner or later. She looked up at the gentleman's face—a Mr. Courtney, she believed he was—and at the definite interest in his eyes. It was, no doubt, because of her dress, scandalous or not. She remembered her resolve to flirt and do her best to make Kenneth jealous, and the little rebellion she felt earlier resurfaced. Kenneth was not here, but at least perhaps she could practice. She smiled at Mr.

Courtney and fluttered her eyelashes as she had seen other ladies do. His eyes grew warmer and he smiled widely. This was much better than facing Lady Hathaway—at least for now, said the rebellion that had grown suddenly larger inside of her.

She danced the next dance and then another; she was suddenly popular for once, and she could not help liking it. Kenneth was not here; why should she not have just a little enjoyment? She caught sight of Lady Hathaway's face again—well, just for a little while, at least.

She could not avoid facing Lady Hathaway forever. The dance ended, and deliberately she walked to her hostess, steeling herself for the lecture she was sure she would receive. She bit her lip and looked down at her hands clutching each other in front of her.

"I am sorry, Lady Hathaway, I meant to tell you—"

"Well, and so I wish you had!" Lady Hathaway said immediately, her voice quite stern. "Lady Quarles has been quizzing me for the last half hour, asking me who your dressmaker is, and where you found the pattern for your dress!"

Aimee looked up, startled. "I thought—"

Lady Hathaway frowned. "You cannot know how awkward it is to have no answer when someone is being so pressing! I do wish you would tell me what you mean to do with your clothes before we go anywhere." She leaned closer to Aimee and said confidentially, "You need not tell me if you do not wish! But I would be grateful if you could tell me which pattern book you used—I must say the dress is excessively becoming!"

Aimee felt oddly deflated. So much for rebellion! Here she had thought she had been horribly fast and daring, only to find she had managed to bring herself up to fashion. It seemed she was, indeed, quite provincial in her tastes.

"Oh, it was only a little alteration, ma'am," she replied as she took the shawl Lady Hathaway held out to her. She pulled it around her shoulders and neck, and she felt almost as if she had pulled a cloak of invisibility over her, for gentlemen passed by her as they often did. "This is the blue sarcenet I chose two weeks ago—do you remember?"

"Yes, indeed I do," Lady Hathaway replied, and began to talk of fashions. Aimee listened, then Psyche drew her mother's attention for Mr. D'Amant had arrived, and at last Aimee sat alone.

Psyche had felt decidedly nervous when she first stepped into Almack's. She had been there many times since the beginning of the Season, of course. The problem was that Harry had not.

No one had ever come into Almack's unless approved by one of the patronesses; she had been lucky that her mother was a friend of one of the Seftons' relatives, and that Cassandra had become amiably acquainted with Lady Cowper. However, as far as Psyche knew, Harry was acquainted with no one in the *ton* outside of her own family, and certainly not with any of the patronesses or their close acquaintances. How horrid it would be if he somehow managed to enter the assembly rooms and was forcibly ejected!

What if Harry made Lady Jersey become truly silent as a stone statue, or turned Princess Lieven into a Gorgon? Or perhaps both? How awkward and uncomfortable it would be if half the guests ran screaming from the rooms, while the other half turned into stone under the princess's baleful eye and snaky brow! The traffic on the street outside was bad enough as it was without such a thing happening. Further, stone statues could possibly be chipped or broken in the panicked rush. She would not like it if any of the patronesses—any person, in fact—became chipped or cracked. How difficult it would be to match the pieces together! And how would she explain any of it, should anyone ask her? No, no, it would never do!

She half hoped that Harry would not appear, and when she had stepped into the ballroom, she was relieved that she did not see him. Well, she could just enjoy dancing and talking with friendly acquaintances, and not worry. She relaxed and looked about her. The assembly room had been decorated this time with large ferns at either side of each window and pots of flowers; someone had apparently decided on a springlike theme this evening, although Psyche could not help thinking that it would be easy to upset the flowerpots should anyone dance too near them.

She caught Aimee's eye and smiled at her. Aimee returned the smile, but it was a worried one, and Psyche felt sure she was wishing that Kenneth was here. Perhaps her brother would arrive—he had said he might, and she believed that he had felt guilty enough about shooting the library wall so that he would make an added effort to come to Almack's in recompense. She clucked her tongue in disapproval at the thought of such damage to a wall. Really, Harry should not have encouraged him to shoot pistols, and she was sure he must have, for he was very fond of shooting things.

On the other hand, she would have much preferred having Harry here than Lieutenant Pargeter. For there was no mistaking him, or the revulsed look that came over his face when he caught sight of her. Psyche turned away quickly, suppressing the laugh that bubbled up inside her but she ended up coughing instead.

"May I have the honor of procuring you some refreshment? You seem to have acquired a cough."

Psyche looked up and almost choked. "Harry! How did

you manage to enter Almack's? I am sure you cannot have received a voucher!"

Harry lifted his chin haughtily. "I am a god. Of course I received a voucher."

"That's all very well, but you must not say such things in company! People will think you quite odd, or at best odiously full of self-consequence."

This time he raised his eyebrows, looking more superior than ever. "It is merely the truth. A god's presence must be accepted anywhere."

"Not at Almack's!" Psyche said, suppressing a rising desire to pinch him. She imagined the look Mrs. Drummond-Burrell could give to an encroaching mushroom and shuddered. No one could be proof against that!

"Even here," Harry said, and said it with such odious arrogance that she stared at him suspiciously. He grinned suddenly. "It was easy, actually. Kenneth and I went to Manton's for target practice and met Lord Jersey there. We walked up Bond Street together where we met Lady Jersey in her carriage. His lordship introduced us, and she was kind enough to offer me a voucher on the spot."

Psyche wrinkled her nose at him. "You toadied to her in a disgusting way, I imagine."

"You wound me, Psyche," Harry said, sighing sadly and shaking his head. "I toady to no one, you know that."

"Hmph. You certainly wheedle—I know you do that."

Harry considered this for a moment. "No, 'wheedle' is too weak a word. 'Excellent powers of persuasion,' is a better phrase. One must have such, you know, to be a god of love."

How impervious to a set-down he was! Psyche sighed and gave it up, then looked at him critically. "You look very well this evening," she said.

"Do you think so?" Harry said, his brow creasing. "I did wish to look well, you know."

Psyche smiled at him and patted his arm comfortingly. "You do, indeed, and you tied your neckcloth quite well. What kind is it? The style, I mean?"

Harry grinned. "The *Trone d'Amour*, of course." Psyche rolled her eyes, but chuckled. He took her hand. "Would you like to dance?"

"Yes, please."

She did so like dancing with him. He was very good at it, and she felt again like she was floating across the floor. But she almost stumbled when he said, "I brought the darts, by the way."

"Did you?" she faltered. "Well, I have been thinking . . . perhaps it would not be a good thing to throw them tonight. Kenneth is not here, after all."

"As you wish." Harry shrugged. "Perhaps you are right—I should do it myself. It did occur to me that you could practice with the darts—just in case your aim is a bit off, that is." He paused for a moment, gazing at her in a considering manner. "Not, of course, that I think you are a bad shot. No, not at all."

"Don't humor me, Harry," Psyche said, grinding her teeth.

He gazed at her admiringly. "How you manage to speak through your teeth like that is quite remarkable. I have never been able to do it without mumbling."

The dance parted them, and Psyche did not have the chance to speak the choice words that almost burst from her. She recovered herself, however, remembering her mother's admonition that a lady tried to keep her conversation pleasant at all times upon the dance floor. Her teeth were still clenched when she came around to Harry again, but she made herself smile around it.

"Dear Harry," she said, her voice as sweet as she could make it. "Do let me try those darts—for practice, as you said."

"My, do I hear you wheedling?"

Psyche wished they were dancing the waltz, for then she could step on his foot with a great deal of force, but unfortunately, it was only a country dance. "*Give me the darts*," she hissed, then remembered her manners. "Please."

"Hmm. Let me think about it," Harry replied.

The dance ended, and he led her to one side of the ballroom near a tall potted palm. "Well?" she demanded. "Have you thought about it yet?"

He opened his hand, revealing a mound of tiny darts, each one not much larger than the size of a bee. "You have to be careful, you know. You need to choose people who are fairly good matches to begin with." He nodded toward the dance floor, where ladies and gentlemen were beginning to line up for a dance set—a waltz. "Miss Samuel and Sir Anthony Bander—the gentleman who looks like he should be a Spanish pirate—for instance. He worships the ground she walks on, but she is just a little frightened of him. There is nothing for her to fear, of course, other than her mother's wish that she would look higher than a baronet. You might try Miss Samuel, just when they are looking at each other."

Psyche looked carefully around her just in case anyone should be looking at her. She selected one of the darts and edging just behind the potted palm, made a quick throw. It missed, hitting an elderly gentleman who was dancing with an equally elderly lady. Psyche grimaced, then shot Harry a defiant look. "I missed, true, but I did hit someone."

"Not a total loss—that's Lord Kitt and his wife; it should only strengthen the affection they already have for each other, and Lady Kitt will soon believe herself to be the luckiest woman alive." He took one of the darts. "Here, let me show you."

With a quick flick of the wrist, he tossed the dart and hit a lady of haughty demeanor just as she took the hand of a sturdy-looking gentleman who looked as if he would have been happier on a farm than a dance floor. Immediately the lady's face softened and she smiled a smile of such sweet invitation at the gentleman that he looked startled and blushed.

"Oh, let me try again! There is Lord Sandringham and Miss Stover—I know they would be perfect for each other," Psyche said, and took another dart. She flicked it in the manner she had seen Harry use, but it did not hit Lord Sandringham but another gentleman. A fierce look passed over that gentleman's face and he pulled his startled partner indecently close to him.

"Heavens!" Psyche said. "I did not mean *that* to happen!"

"I'm sure they will do quite well together," Harry said. There seemed to be a tremor of laughter in his voice, but when she looked at him, he was looking with bland interest at the dancers in front of them, as if picking out the next potential couple. "And look—it seems your brother has come after all."

He had indeed. Kenneth was looking particularly fine in his regimentals, and had taken Aimee to the dance floor and was waltzing with her. There seemed a little uncertainty between them, as if they were not quite comfortable dancing with each other, though both of them danced very well. Perhaps it was in the way they danced so far apart—perfectly proper, of course, but at arm's length away. Psyche thought of how the one gentleman she had shot had brought his partner so very close to him . . . it would not be a terribly scandalous thing if Kenneth happened to do the same thing, for he and Aimee were betrothed, after all. And since these were just little darts, and Kenneth was at this time enamored of the portrait, perhaps it would have just the right effect on him.

"Well, since Kenneth is here and dancing with Aimee, it cannot hurt to try to get it over with and hit him with a dart, can it?" she said. "He is not all that far away from us—surely I could hit him from here."

"I am sure you are right," Harry said, and this time he had a wide grin on his face when she glanced at him.

"I *will* hit him, you know," Psyche said, frowning at him.

"Did I say you would not?"

"No. . . ."

"And you have practiced quite a few times already, have you not?"

"Yes. . . ."

"Well, then!" Harry said, putting more darts into her hand. "There you are—you may begin at anytime."

Psyche gave one last long look at him, which he returned with an expectant air, before she turned toward the dancers in front of her. There! Kenneth was quite close now. With a quick flick of her wrist and fingers, she tossed the dart at him.

It missed. Instead, it hit a gentleman to the left of him, who immediately twirled his partner off the dance floor and sank to his knees at her feet.

"Amanda, my heart! Say you will be mine forever!" he said soulfully. A few shrieks of laughter sounded from around him and the lady's face grew red.

"Really, Sir James, *do* get up!" she cried, clearly flustered.

Psyche winced. "Oh, dear. I did not mean that to happen."

"Never mind," Harry replied, and patted her hand. "I will attend to it. Do continue and try to hit your brother."

Psyche stared hard at Kenneth; she would get him this

time, certainly. Perhaps if she tossed it in an underhand throw, it would work better.

She missed. "Heavens, this is difficult!" she muttered. "I do wish they would not move about so!" Another glance at Harry showed him grinning wider than ever. How infuriating! She *would* do it right—he'd see!

Somehow, however, she did not, and soon the dancers began weaving about the dance floor in an alarming way. There was Mr. Compton and Miss Aubrey dancing so close to each other that they seemed to be made of one piece—and was Lord Hamilton actually *kissing* Lady Anne Brandon? Titters and scandalized shrieks began to rise in the ballroom, and when Psyche glanced across the room, she could see Lady Jersey staring in confusion at the dancers, while Princess Lieven's face grew stiff with disapproval. Lady Hathaway was sitting next to Lady Sefton, and Psyche saw her mother look up and hastily rise from her chair and walk toward her, clearly determined to take her away from a place that was beginning to look more like a den of iniquity than Almack's. Psyche stared at the remaining darts in her hand. Surely she would be able to get Kenneth with one of them before her mother came? She could hardly wish to be caught with them in her hands! She took in a deep breath. Very well then!

Kenneth and Aimee came near, and Psyche saw her chance—with a desperate fling, she threw all four darts toward the couple at once.

"What *are* you doing, Psyche?" Lady Hathaway demanded.

"Oh . . . oh, my hand seemed to get a cramp, Mama, so I thought I should shake it out a little," Psyche said. Which was, actually, the truth, for it had been getting a little stiff from all the throwing, she thought. She would hardly wish to lie to her mother, after all!

"Well, I wish you would not do it in such an obvious fashion, my dear. But that is neither here nor there!" Lady Hathaway gazed sternly at the remaining dancers straggling upon the dance floor. "I must say this is *not* the sort of behavior I expected at Almack's, and you may be sure I told Lady Sefton so! Though not in those words of course! Indeed, I think perhaps we should cut short this evening—I am beginning to think it is not lemonade that was served this night, and I should hardly wish you to begin acting in such a manner as well, Psyche."

"But I wouldn't—"

"Never mind! I have decided we shall go home, and Aimee can go home with Kenneth, as he has said he would escort her tonight."

"But *they* are not leaving," Psyche protested.

"*They* are betrothed, and may do as they like—as long as Aimee comes home at a reasonable hour," Lady Hathaway said complacently. "Besides, they seem to be getting along quite amiably at the moment; I should hardly wish to interrupt it."

Psyche looked at her brother and Aimee, and frowned. It seemed she had not hit Kenneth at all, for he looked no different from the way he had before, and Aimee's whole demeanor was still uncomfortable. It seemed she had hit some other people, however—Pargeter among them, for he was staring at someone on the dance floor with great intensity, though she could not see who it was. Well, she was glad of that! Perhaps he would stay away from Aimee in that case. She turned and caught sight of Harry, leaning against the wall and surveying the ballroom, a mischievous smile on his face. She glanced at the remaining dancers and drew in a dismayed breath.

To their credit, the musicians in the balcony above had not let the disorder below them distract their playing and had continued valiantly. There were, perhaps three pairs of dancers left who twirled around in some semblance of order. The rest seemed to be in one sort of disarray or another; some couples had ceased dancing altogether. A few were in corners, standing far too close together; and it seemed Lord Hamilton had not stopped kissing Miss Brandon, even though both their mothers were tugging at their arms.

Psyche looked back at Harry and saw that his shoulders were shaking and his lips were pressed together as if suppressing laughter. The suspicion she'd felt earlier suddenly bloomed into realization—he had *meant* her to throw the darts all along! Oh, how odious he was! She turned away and followed her mother out of the ballroom. When she saw Harry next, she would—she would—

She did not know what she would do, but it would *not* be pleasant!

Aimee watched just a little wistfully as Psyche and Mr. D'Amant went off to dance the country dance. She did not mind sitting one out, for her feet ached a little with the dancing she had done already, but Kenneth did say he might come to Almack's this time, and she so wished he would come soon. Mr. Pargeter was here, and she thought he might ask her to dance but he merely bowed and turned away. She watched him for a moment, and saw him gazing at Psyche with a look of revulsion, while Psyche wore an expression of cheerful politeness. Something must have happened between the two, for she could not conceive of anyone thinking of her friend in anything but the most pleasant way. Psyche was a cheerful and friendly girl, and pretty besides, and whose sense of humor was quite delightful. Perhaps Lieutenant Pargeter did not share the same sense of humor as Psyche, and had been put off by one of her jokes. Although she could not think how anything Psyche might have said would make him look at her so.

Aimee sighed, pulling her shawl more closely around her neck and shoulders. She opened her fan, running her fingers over the details of the painting on it, showing the mythological figures of Pygmalion and Galatea. Kenneth had given it to her not long ago. She had been pleased and touched by the gift, for it was a beautiful thing with ivory handles and made of delicate silk. But now she gazed at the picture and felt almost as if she were as set in her place as the statue of Galatea, not able to move from the pedestal that Kenneth had set her on, for all that he claimed to adore her. One did not dance with a statue, did one? Perhaps that was why Kenneth was not here now. Her dress alteration had been for nothing.

Oh, yes, *do* talk yourself into a blue megrim, Aimee Mattingly! she told herself sternly. Did he not kiss you at the Conningtons' ball? A man does not do *that* with a statue! But he had withdrawn from her later, and it seemed as if the wall was back between them as soon as they had returned into the light of the ballroom. He had looked at her in a puzzled way, as if he could not make the connection between the Aimee he had kissed in the darkness of the garden and the woman he saw before him in the light of the chandeliers.

Aimee pressed her lips together firmly. She had worn a daring new dress and had flirted madly as she dared, but he was not here to see it. The uncertainty was wearing on her, and sometimes she felt she could not stand the way he seemed to blow hot and cold upon her. They would go to the country soon, however, and there perhaps she would find out what was bothering Kenneth so. She knew something must be, for though he would not speak of it, she could almost feel the tension coming from him. Her own body tensed in response to it.

As it did now. She looked up, and there was Kenneth smiling down at her. She could not help the glad leaping of her heart at the sight of him, or the concern that followed so closely when she saw how tired he looked.

He took her hand. "A dance, Aimee?" he asked.

"Perhaps . . . perhaps you would prefer to sit with me, Kenneth? You do look a little tired," she said.

His hand tightened on hers. "I am *not* tired, I assure you," he said, and smiled in a tight, almost defiant way.

Aimee gazed at him and knew that to insist otherwise would anger him, and she did not wish for any display of it, not here in Almack's. "Very well," she said, rose from her chair, and dropped the shawl from her shoulders.

His steps did not falter as the other gentlemen had when they looked upon her nearly unclad bosom. He gave her only one brief glance as he led her in the steps of the dance, and his hand held hers firmly. He danced with less grace than he was used to, and held himself stiffly, as if his shoulders bore some invisible weight upon them. Her alteration had no effect on him at all. Aimee closed her eyes in despair.

"Kenneth, this is nonsense," she said abruptly. He raised his brows at her, but she continued quickly, hastily, so that she would not take back the words now that she began. "You *are* tired, though you deny it. You need not have come here, and yes, I am glad you did, but it is stupid to dance when you should be sleeping." And when you clearly have no interest in me, she thought, but could not quite bring herself to say it.

"I sleep at least ten hours a day, if you must know," Kenneth said and smiled ruefully. "That is more than enough for anyone."

Aimee shook her head. "Not if you are tired still. Or perhaps you are ill—"

"No, I am not ill, either!" he replied, his voice clearly

irritable. "Will you stop? I have had enough of coddling from my mother, I need not have it from you, too."

"I am sorry if you do not wish me to care for you, Kenneth, but I can't help but speak when you don't look well."

Kenneth raised his chin, and looked past her, closing his lips firmly. It was clear that he would not speak further of it, and Aimee's stomach burned with both anger and frustration. For now it mattered less to her whether he still loved her or not. His well-being was more important. What would it take to make him listen? She did not want him to be driven to a state of collapse, and yet something seemed to push him onward regardless. Perhaps he would listen to his father . . . but she doubted it; even though she could clearly see the love and pride Sir John had for his son, Kenneth could not seem to see it.

She turned the conversation toward more mundane subjects, and his tight-lipped expression relaxed. But his back was still stiff, his conversation desultory, and Aimee knew his attention was elsewhere, not here with her.

Lieutenant Pargeter scanned the crowd closest to him for a likely dance partner, and for a moment his eye lighted on Miss Hathaway and he shuddered. The memory of his plunge, naked, into the Conningtons' icy moat was painfully fresh in his mind, and though he still could not discern how his clothes had disappeared, he was certain Miss Hathaway had something to do with it. It was best that he not go near her at all—indeed, he was beginning to think that the sight of the Hathaway family boded ill for him. It was, of course, nonsense, but he could not help feeling that misfortune followed them, in particular when he was about. Besides, Miss Hathaway was with that D'Amant puppy, who made him feel damnably uncomfortable with that knowing look he had about him. At the moment they seemed to be tossing something at the dancers—an odd pair, to be sure, and he was better off avoiding them altogether.

He gazed past Miss Hathaway to Miss Aimee Mattingly, who sat in her chair, looking at once anxious and wistful. She was a pretty little thing, her charms more bounteous than he'd imagined, and it would be a coup to snatch her out from under Captain Hathaway's nose, but he also remembered Miss Hathaway's warning and that uncomfortable moment when he had to decide between facing the captain and jumping over the balcony into the moat. Since he was always a good man to chart out the best strategies on the battlefield, he knew that a strategic retreat in that case had been the best choice.

In fact, it would be a good thing to give up his obsession about Captain Hathaway's unfair elevation into a captaincy. Pargeter leaned against the wall and frowned thoughtfully. He admitted it: he had been obsessed. There were other ways to rise in the world, after all, and surely he was large-minded enough to forgive and forget? Yes, it would be best to avoid the Hathaways altogether—they were too troublesome by half. All he needed to do was look about him for a suitable heiress, for example, and certainly he was well-favored enough to attract one. And there! Captain Hathaway had come to Almack's after all, and had taken his bride-to-be up for the waltz. It would never do to part a couple that was clearly meant for each other.

Lieutenant Pargeter smiled pleasantly. Truly, he was a generous-minded man, and it was too bad that more people did not realize it. He gazed at Miss Mattingly, following her progress around the ballroom, and could not help wishing just a little wistfully that she might know what she had missed in preferring Kenneth Hathaway to him.

For a moment he thought he saw some sort of insect coming toward him—nonsense, for bees did not come out at night. But a sudden stinging sensation pricked him somewhere in the region of his heart, and it seemed he could not look away from Miss Mattingly. He swallowed, and a quick, jealous anger went through him. Why did not Miss Mattingly prefer him to Hathaway? She *should* prefer him, Francis Pargeter, a man far superior to Kenneth Hathaway, or indeed any of the Hathaway clan. Indeed, she was wasted on that fool—she, who was the most beautiful woman he'd ever seen. He pushed himself from the ballroom wall and took a step toward the dancing pair. A part of him hesitated, ringing alarm bells frantically in his head and screaming, *no, no you said you wouldn't go near Hathaway you idiot—he's a madman!* But he was sure it was the base, cowardly part of him— not that he had a base, cowardly part, but whatever it was, it would not keep him from going to the woman with whom he knew he was irretrievably, absolutely in love.

He cared not that it was simply not done for anyone to cut into a dance, he cared not that he might be censured for causing a scene on the dance floor. No, that Hathaway even dared touch that angel's hand was an abomination, and not to be borne. Swiftly his legs took his raging body, his enamored heart, and his agitated and protesting brain to his goddess's side, and he stopped the dancing pair with a firm hand.

"My dance, I believe?" he said pleasantly to Miss Mattingly.

"What the blo—devil take it, Pargeter, what is the meaning of this?" Captain Hathaway said.

Again Pargeter hesitated, the little screaming voice within him giving him pause, but he pushed it nobly aside, despite feeling oddly like a puppet pulled here and there by some invisible string. "You, sir, are not fit to touch the hem of this lady's gown. That she allows a dance with her admirers is a privilege that should be reserved for those who deserve her—as you, sir—" The little voice inside him groaned dolorously. "As you sir, do not."

"That may be," Captain Hathaway said, eyeing him up and down. "But I think it's for the lady to say, not you."

"You are offensive, sir!"

"I? I think it's the other way around, Pargeter!"

"Please, for heaven's sake, don't argue like this, not here!" Aimee cried, tugging at Kenneth's arm. He pulled away from her.

"There!" Pargeter said, bending an angry eye at Kenneth. "You cannot even treat her with the gentleness that she deserves. I should call you out for that!"

"Deuce take it, I should call *you* out for that insult! As if I would—damn, Pargeter are you disguised?"

The lieutenant sneered. "Not I! But I would—"

"Not here!" Aimee said again. "Please! Oh, Kenneth, take me home!"

"*I* shall take you home, Miss Mattingly," the lieutenant said, glaring at Kenneth.

"The devil you will," Kenneth replied, and took Aimee's hand. "Come, Aimee."

Aimee looked at both of the men, and drew away from them. "No," she said. "I will not go with either of you. I will find Lady Hathaway, or Cassandra, and I will leave here now."

"But—"

"Aimee—"

"No!" she cried, and turned away, her face hot with blushes. She was sure the whole assembly must be staring at her and could not look up at anyone as she rushed from the dance floor. Hastily she searched for Lady Hathaway and saw them both go out the door and almost ran to them.

"Lady Hathaway . . . Psyche!" The two ladies turned and looked at her.

"What is it, my dear?" Lady Hathaway said, her brow creased in concern.

"Please, I wish to leave with you—I have the headache, and . . . and Kenneth is occupied at the moment."

"But I thought—" Lady Hathaway said, glancing back at her son. "Heavens! What is he doing with Lieutenant Pargeter?"

"He . . . he is talking to him, ma'am."

"It looks like he wishes to strangle him, frankly, and that will never do! I must go to him and—"

"No, no, please, Lady Hathaway, let us go. I swear I never wish to see either of them again!" Aimee said passionately.

Psyche seemed to gaze at a point past the two arguing men, and Aimee saw that she was giving one last look at Mr. D'Amant, who shrugged, then walked toward the two men.

Lady Hathaway gazed at her for a long moment, then nodded. "Very well, then." She held out her hand to Aimee and nodded at Psyche. "Let us go. The carriage is waiting for us. And since it seems that Mr. D'Amant is speaking sensibly to both of them—a very pleasant, charming young man, Psyche, I must say! I do not see why you are not more pleasant to him—I believe we might leave without any worry that they might come to fisticuffs. This is Almack's, after all! One does not do such things in this place. Although," she said, pulling her shawl closer about her and shaking her head, "I must say this has been a very strange evening! Everyone has acted in such an odd manner—and heavens, Lord Hamilton and

Miss Brandon! To think I had always thought them such a perfectly well-brought up pair! Not that they would not make an excellent match, to be sure, which is just as well, since there is no doubt that they will be wed whether they like it or not. Not that I think they do not like it, if such a scandalous display of, of, well, affection, is any indication!"

Aimee pulled her own shawl closer about her, and listened to Lady Hathaway's chatter, trying to take some comfort from the familiarity of it. A hand touched her shoulder, and she looked up to see Psyche gazing at her with deep concern.

"Oh, Aimee, I am so sorry!"

"Why?" Aimee smiled slightly. "I doubt their argument will come to anything. They can hardly come to fisticuffs at Almack's, after all."

"I . . . I suppose I could have watched Kenneth a little better," Psyche faltered.

"Nonsense! He is not a child, after all," Lady Hathaway said, and patted Psyche's hand kindly. "Really, love, you had nothing to do with it, and you take these things too much to heart. Nothing will come of it, I am sure."

Psyche gave her mother a weak smile and fell silent. But Aimee did not pay much attention to Psyche's unusual silence though she wondered at it. Doubt troubled Aimee's mind, and she wondered whether it would be best to go back to her uncle's house in the country instead of staying with the Hathaways. Not that she wasn't grateful, of course, and she had come to love them as her own family. But she was beginning to think that perhaps it would be best for her and Kenneth to part, at least for a little while. She was tired of waiting and tired of trying to get Kenneth to speak of what burdens he was carrying, and her change in dress and manners improved nothing at all. Perhaps it was a weakness in herself—but if that were so, then perhaps she should let another, more persistent, woman become Kenneth's wife. A sharp ache in her chest made her draw in a sobbing breath, but she swallowed down the tears that came with it. She loved him still, but now she wondered if perhaps she was not the best wife for him. If so, it would be best if he found another.

One more week she would try—she could not help extending it—and then she would go home. Meanwhile, she would return to the Hathaways' town house, get a good night's rest, and hopefully be able to think more clearly the next morning.

# Chapter 8

[faint mirrored text from previous page bleeding through]

**H**owever, neither Aimee nor the rest of the Hathaway household would be able to rest easy that night. For when Lady Hathaway and her charges stepped into the house, they were met by an extremely wooden-faced butler.

"What is it, Trimble?" Lady Hathaway said anxiously. "Has Sir John sent a message that he is ill? I knew he should not have gone to Edinburgh to search out that Greek manuscript! He never travels well, you know."

"No, my lady, it is not Sir John." Trimble's face grew more stiff than ever.

"Cassandra, then? Is she having trouble with her condition?"

"No, my lady, it is not Lady Blytheland."

"Then is it Kenneth?"

He hesitated, then glanced at Aimee and Psyche. "I would not like to say in front of the young ladies."

"It *is* Kenneth, then," Psyche said instantly, "but you know we will find out sooner or later, so you might as well say it, Trimble."

"Hush, Psyche!" Lady Hathaway said, then turned to the butler. "He is not involved in a duel, is he?"

"No, my lady."

"Well, heavens, it cannot be very bad, then. Tell us!"

Trimble looked past Lady Hathaway, and his face

worked in a way that made Aimee think that he had intense indigestion. Finally he sighed and said, "There is a Young Person who has called upon us, asking for the young master Kenneth."

"And what does he want with Kenneth?" Lady Hathaway asked.

An expression of acute pain came over Trimble's face. "It is not a *he*, my lady, but a *she*."

Aimee took in a slow breath and closed her eyes briefly. No, really, it was probably nothing. Kenneth would never have betrayed their betrothal.

"She?" Lady Hathaway said, then looked at Aimee. "Aimee, do go up and get yourself ready for your bed—this has been quite a fatiguing evening, to be sure! And Psyche, do go up with her."

"I'm sorry, ma'am," Aimee said. "I think I should like to hear what this lady has to say regarding Kenneth. If it concerns him, it concerns me, also."

Lady Hathaway sighed. "Very well. Trimble, have this young lady go to the drawing room, if you please! We shall be there shortly." Trimble bowed and left, and Lady Hathaway walked down the hall. "Heavens, as if the events at Almack's were not fatiguing enough we must have this! I am sure it is nothing, of course. It is probably some little matter, easily cleared up." She pushed open the drawing room door, sat down on a chair, and waved Aimee toward the sofa. She gazed at Psyche. "What, are you still here? I thought I told you to go upstairs!"

"I mean to be a prop to Aimee," Psyche said firmly.

"Nonsense!" her mother replied. "I shall—"

But then the door opened, and Trimble announced, "Miss Mary Rivers, my lady."

A cloaked figure almost stumbled into the room, hesitated, then came forward. A small hand pushed back the hood, revealing a pretty, dark-haired girl with delicate features. "I—I am sorry, but would Lieutenant Hathaway be here?" Her voice was well-bred, and musical—not common at all, as Aimee had hoped. She had a sweet face, and lips that looked as if they would be inclined to smile if they were not drooping now with weariness. Miss Rivers hesitated and drew in a deep breath. "I have heard that this is his home, and . . . and I have not heard from him in a long time. I took the money he left me and came here, hoping to see him. I would like to speak to him, if I may."

Lady Hathaway looked at the girl and if Aimee had not known her hostess for the kind lady she was, she would have thought her a cold-hearted matron from the freezing look she gave Miss Rivers. "I am Lady Hathaway, *Captain* Hathaway's mother. He is not here. If there is anything you wish to say to him, you may say it to me."

The girl closed her eyes in apparent despair. "It's been so long," she whispered. She opened her eyes again and tried to smile. "Is he a captain now? I am not surprised. He is very brave, I know. Please, if you would give me his direction, I will find him."

"I think perhaps you should state your business with him to me, first," Lady Hathaway said.

The girl lifted her chin. "I am sorry, my lady, but my business is with him. I do not wish to disturb you any more than you already have been."

Lady Hathaway's lips thinned in displeasure. "I am not at all inclined to tell you where he is quartered."

The girl looked almost as if she would weep, but sighed deeply instead. "In that case, I will search further, and give you good night," she said, and curtsied. She turned swiftly, but suddenly gave a low moan and sank slowly to her knees and then to the floor in a faint.

"Oh, heavens!" Lady Hathaway cried, and rushed to her side. She picked up her wrist and felt her brow. "She is ill, poor thing! Psyche, ring for Trimble. Oh, dear, how awkward. I cannot think—oh, dear, oh dear. Whoever she may be or whatever she wants, we cannot just toss her out the door. Trimble, there you are! Have a footman carry Miss Rivers to the yellow room."

Aimee stared at the young woman, half in pity, half in anguish. Was this, perhaps, why Kenneth had acted so strangely? The girl was no common woman from the streets—it was clear from her accent and her manner. It would explain everything—the way he did not say the sweet words he used to say before the war, the exaggerated avowals of devotion. Exaggerated because they came from a false or guilty heart, she was sure.

But you don't know this, said the rational part of herself. The girl hasn't said what her purpose in wishing to see Kenneth is. Aimee held to the thought as if it was a buoy to keep her above the turbulent feelings that threatened to wash over her. She watched as a strong footman picked up the girl as if she were featherlight and carried her out of the room. Lady Hathaway followed, wringing her hands anxiously. Slowly Aimee rose from her chair and went toward the door.

"Aimee."

She turned and looked at Psyche.

"Aimee, I am sure it is nothing. You know Kenneth would not have, he couldn't . . ." Psyche gazed at her anxiously.

"Perhaps," Aimee said, and made her clenched hands relax. "I suppose we shall find out soon." She turned, went out the door, and ran upstairs.

When Psyche went up to her room after Aimee left her, she retained enough control over herself to dismiss her maid after she undressed and put on her dressing gown. Then she took a small china vase and threw it against the hearth with all her might. It broke with a very satisfying crash, and she smiled fiercely. Then she closed her eyes and said quietly through her teeth: "Harry, I want you here *now*! At this minute, do you hear me?" She opened her eyes and tapped her foot impatiently.

A soft glow appeared at her window, and she opened it. Slowly, the glow drifted through it and down to the floor. It grew taller, but did not quite take shape, seeming almost to hesitate.

"Now!" Psyche repeated.

"Oh, very well!" With a bright flash, Harry appeared before her, dressed in his usual chiton and with his arms crossed over his chest. He leaned a shoulder against one newel of the mantelpiece and looked down his nose at her.

"Don't you look at me like that—as if there was something I have done wrong!" Psyche snapped. "You *knew* I would hit the wrong people! You let me throw those darts because you wished to cause havoc at Almack's!"

Harry looked bored and traced his index finger over a piece of carved molding on the mantelpiece ledge. "Well, you must admit you insisted you could do it—and I believed you, of course."

Psyche felt a pang of guilt—it was true that she had begged him to let her try. But that was not the whole of it. "I don't think you really did believe me—you were humoring me, I am sure! And now that I think of it, you could have stopped me after my first few tries, and not only that, you could have hit Kenneth yourself, but you didn't even throw one dart at him."

Harry rolled his eyes in impatience. "Come now, Psyche, didn't you think it was just a little bit entertaining? Perhaps I didn't think you as sure a shot as I—well, who could be? But I thought I ought to let you try. And I thought it quite amusing to have people stumbling about on the dance floor."

"Not at Almack's! I dread to think what the patronesses must think of tonight's events."

"There have been five betrothal announcements tonight, and I can assure you that Lady Jersey considers this evening to be a signal success," Harry said, grinning at her.

"But *I* do not! Not where Aimee and Kenneth are concerned. I am afraid that Lieutenant Pargeter was hit, and has formed a passion for Aimee now, and his argument with Kenneth has upset her dreadfully."

Harry looked uncomfortable. "Well, it will come to nothing, I am sure."

Psyche eyed him closely. He had a defiant look in his eyes, but his wings drooped in a suspicious manner. "There's more to it than that, isn't there?" She crossed her arms in front of her. "Tell me!"

He gave an impatient sigh. "If you must know, they are going to fight a duel tomorrow morning."

Dread made her stomach ache, and she stared at him, her hand rising to her lips. "Oh, no, Harry. Oh, please, no!"

"It will come to nothing, I assure you. It will be twenty-five paces, and your brother is an excellent shot, much better than Lieutenant Pargeter. It will be at dawn, at Hyde Park." He shrugged. "Kenneth will come to no harm."

"You can't be sure of that!" Psyche began to pace the floor. "I remember the effect of your arrows, and if the darts are anything like them, Pargeter will feel compelled to do something foolish. Or Kenneth! Nothing good will come of this, I know! If Kenneth kills Pargeter, then he will have to leave the country. And if Pargeter kills Kenneth, then how will that have solved the problem between him and Aimee?" She turned to Harry and gazed at him reproachfully. "Oh, Harry, how could you?"

"*I* did not carelessly throw a dart at Lieutenant Pargeter—you did. And I never said you should shoot anyone while they were dancing—you decided to do that yourself."

Anger flashed suddenly through Psyche. Obviously, Harry was not going to take responsibility for any of it. "You *could* have told me, but you didn't! You, with all your thousands of years of experience should have known what I might have done, but you didn't stop me! Indeed, I think you egged me on."

"I? Egged you on?" Harry put a hand on his chest and raised his brows. "How did I do that?"

"By telling me that you believed me when I said I could shoot—Well, you said it in a way that made me think you thought I couldn't, and I wanted to prove— Oh!" Psyche let out an impatient breath. "You are impossible! Indeed, I think perhaps you wished to give me a set-down, which is why you let me throw those darts."

He smirked, and she wished her parents had not raised her to abhor violence, because she badly wanted to hit him at the moment. But she forced herself to think of Kenneth and the harm that could come to him. "But that is not of importance right now. What we should do is stop the duel."

Harry looked uncomfortable again and moved from the mantelpiece to look out of the window at the night sky, his wings folded behind him. "I am afraid I cannot do that."

"Why not?"

"Well, Kenneth asked me to be his second, and I agreed."

"You what?!" Psyche shrieked.

"He asked me to be his second and—"

"I know what you said—oh, heavens. Oh, dear." Psyche sat down abruptly on her bed and put her hands over her face for a moment. Then she raised her head and looked at him fiercely. "You *will* put a stop to this! If you are his second, you may talk to Pargeter's second and try to persuade Pargeter and Kenneth to stop this duel."

"If you must know, I already tried that," Harry said, hunching his shoulders. "They still will not."

"Then you can use your powers to stop them—leave out the shot or something like that?"

"No. They would know, and it's against their code of honor."

"But I don't care for that!" Psyche said passionately. "I just want my brother alive!"

Harry turned swiftly toward her, frowning. "You said I should come to know mortals more, and I am trying. I have learned there are certain rules you mortals go by, and that one must adhere to them or be thought a coward or less than honorable. Your brother would rather die than be branded either of those things. If I were to make the shot disappear from the pistols, Pargeter would be swift to call him a coward, and they would fight again, and it would be worse." His expression softened and he took her hand and squeezed it. "I am sorry, Psyche. I . . . I will admit I should not have let you throw the darts—I thought it would be amusing, and frankly it was for a while. But I never thought they would wish to fight a duel. I will do my best to keep either of them from being hurt." He sighed. "The best I could do is to change the course of the shots a little and graze both of them slightly. Then both of them would be satisfied."

"But what if you miss?" Psyche cried.

He looked at her straight in the eyes. "I will not, I promise you."

"But what if you make a mistake?"

"I don't—"

"Yes you do! Don't tell me that you don't make mistakes!" Psyche said angrily and stamped her foot. "Not when Kenneth's life is at stake."

As he stared at her, Harry's face grew stony. "You go over the line too many times, Psyche. You do not know everything."

"I may not, but you certainly don't either!" she said. She could feel her face heat with impatience and rage. She knew the stories of how mortals were changed into animals and such when they displeased the Greek gods, and knew there was perhaps some danger there, but she had worked herself up into a passion and she could not stop now. "And I don't care if you are a god or not, or if you or anyone else wishes to punish me for some sort of *hubris,* all I care about is that Kenneth is safe!"

Harry's lips pressed together in a thin hard line. "You don't trust me."

"And why should I? You delight in playing tricks, I know you do."

"I will do as I say," he said through clenched teeth.

Psyche smiled at him fiercely. "My, it seems you do know how to talk through your teeth very well."

With one blazing look and a bright burst of light, Harry disappeared out the window. Psyche sat down abruptly on her bed. Oh, heavens. What had she done? She groaned and put her hands over her face. She should not have lost her temper, but she had been *so* angry! It was her red hair, she was sure. Everyone knew that people with red hair had horrid tempers.

Harry said he would make sure Kenneth was not killed—but she could not be sure of that now, for she had clearly got him angry. Psyche swallowed down her tears. She did not like to get Harry angry, not because she thought he would punish her—he never did—but she missed him sorely when he was not about. He was her best friend, after all.

She drew in a deep breath. Well, there was nothing for it but to do what she could herself, just in case Harry was angry enough not to help. And then, too, she had to admit she was partly at fault. If she had not let herself become irritated at Harry's apparent disbelief in her ability to throw darts, this would not have happened. She should not let him provoke her, but for some reason he always could.

She glanced at the clock and saw that it was quite a bit past midnight. She knew how to wake herself up at a certain time, if she just concentrated on it, no matter how late she got to bed—whenever she told herself the time she'd wake up over and over again before she went to sleep, she always woke up around that time. The maids were always up before dawn, so she could ask one of them to go with her to Hyde Park in the morning.

Psyche crawled into the bed and rubbed her cold feet together to warm them. She murmured the time she would wake up over and over again, and slowly fell asleep.

Aimee could not sleep at all. Images of Kenneth and the pretty young Mary Rivers mixed in her head and made her want to weep. But she swallowed down one lump after another in her throat until she felt there was a big lump in her stomach instead, leaden and aching. She dozed perhaps for a little while, but dreamed of nothing but Kenneth and the tired, distant look he often had, and heard whispers of worship but not of love. Finally she awoke, and it was still dark, but she knew dawn was coming—she could hear the slow movement of servants in the hallway, and the night sky had a rim of light just at the edge of it.

She was tired. Perhaps if she went down to the kitchens and drank some warm milk she would be able to go back to sleep. She got up and put on her dressing gown, then made a little fire with the tinderbox and lit a candle. Then she opened the door of her chamber. A small shriek made her jump as she stepped out of the room.

"Oh! Aimee!" Psyche waved her hand in front of her face and breathed a sigh of relief. "It's only you."

"What are you doing up this early?" Aimee asked, for Psyche was fully clothed.

Psyche hesitated and stared at her for a long moment, then nodded. "I am going to make sure Kenneth does not get killed in a duel."

It was as if all the breath had suddenly left her lungs, and Aimee put her hand upon the wall to steady herself. "A duel?"

"Yes, he is fighting a duel with Lieutenant Pargeter . . . and I think you should come with me. You should be able to persuade him better than I."

Aimee stared at her friend for a long moment. "Of course. Please—please wait." Quickly she ran into her room and pulled out a dress and pelisse and hastily dragged them on. One ribbon was awry and she looked more like a bedraggled waif than a lady of fashion, but she did not care. She ran out of her room again, and grasped Psyche's hand. "Let us go, now! Oh, my dear God. I hope we are not too late. A coach—"

"I've already called for one," Psyche said, and both of them ran down the hall.

The light grew steadily brighter over the trees in Hyde Park, but the air grew no more warm, but was chill and damp, though there were no clouds in the sky. Kenneth shivered and closed his eyes. God, he was tired. He had almost turned over in his bed and had gone back to sleep, but of course he could not do that, not when he had a duel to attend. He was not a coward, and he'd seen more danger than this before. A brief image of himself dead on the grass flickered through his mind, and the thought that it was very like sleep almost settled into him, but he shook himself and scanned the road by the park for a carriage. Pargeter should be here soon. He caught Harry's eye and smiled briefly at him, but it seemed the young man was not inclined to make conversation, for he only gazed at him solemnly and nodded.

The noise of coach wheels caught his attention and he turned—yes, that was Pargeter's carriage, a damned prissy thing of primrose yellow. The lieutenant stumbled out—it seemed the man was as tired as he was. Good. A brief, frightened look crossed Pargeter's face and Kenneth grinned. That was good, also.

He watched as Harry and Pargeter's second inspected the guns—he wished they'd hurry up about it. Each nodded and then turned, presenting the pistols to the opponents. Kenneth took his and weighed it in his hand. It was German-made and seemed well constructed, but he could not be sure whether it would shoot straight or not. Only the most expensive could be relied on to do that, and even then one had to be sure it was custom made. He didn't want to kill the man, just graze him. He wasn't so foolish as to risk exile.

He bowed to the lieutenant, noting the panicked look in the man's eye, and felt a little better. He doubted that Pargeter would hit him, not if he were this nervous. He, Kenneth, was not nervous at all. He closed his eyes for a brief moment as the count began and he stepped away from Pargeter the requisite twenty-five paces. No, he was not nervous, but he was bone tired and felt as if he did not care if he were hit. It would be a relief to lie down and rest and not feel compelled to rise again for a while.

Twenty-five. He turned, faced the lieutenant, and raised the gun, then brought it down again, his finger squeezing the trigger.

"Kenneth!" screamed a female voice. "No, Kenneth, don't!"

He jerked his head to look—Aimee. And then a loud report sounded, his head seemed to burst into fireworks, and then there was only darkness.

# Chapter 9

Aimee leaped down from the carriage and ran to Kenneth, tumbling down beside his still form. He was pale and his temple was bleeding horribly.

"Oh, please God, no. No, Kenneth, you can't be dead!" Her throat was tight and the words came out as a strangled whisper. She pulled out her handkerchief and pressed it upon the wound—useless, for it was a tiny thing, easily soaked with his blood and the tears that fell from her face. She pulled up her skirts and tore off the cotton flounce from her petticoat and pressed that upon his head.

"Here, take this and tie it about his head to hold the pad steady." She looked up to see Psyche—pale and trembling—handing her another length of cotton, apparently from her petticoat, as well. Carefully she took the cotton and wrapped it around Kenneth's head.

Someone bent down next to her—Mr. D'Amant, Psyche's beau. He put his hand under Kenneth's chin, and Kenneth flinched as if his touch stung him. "He is alive, and I believe he only has a graze upon his head. You must not fret, Miss Mattingly. Head wounds always bleed very freely." For a moment he stared at Psyche, his lips pressed tightly together. "I thought I told you—" he said, but stopped. Psyche looked away from him.

"Aimee. . . ."

"Kenneth!" Aimee took his face in her hands and kissed him. "Kenneth!"

For one moment he opened his eyes and stared at her as if he had never seen her before, and then his lips relaxed in a smile. "My love," he said. "My sweet Aimee." His eyes closed again.

"Come," Mr. D'Amant said. "Let us take him home in the carriage." He flicked the fingers of one hand as if tossing something, then signaled to Pargeter's second, a stout young man of dandified appearance, who blenched before he came forward. Together they lifted Kenneth and put him in the coach.

A loud cry came from the field and Aimee looked quickly toward the sound. Lieutenant Pargeter stared at them, and if Aimee had not been so filled with dread and anguish for Kenneth, she would have laughed, for the lieutenant's face was the picture of astonishment and confusion.

"By damn!" he said. "I hit him! With nary a scratch on me."

A small growl came from beside her, and Aimee looked up to see fury on Psyche's face. "Your arm is bleeding, Lieutenant!" she called to him. The man looked down and spotted the red that was seeping through his coat sleeve. He paled and closed his eyes.

"Anderson! Come quickly! I've been wounded, and my coat—! I just bought it yesterday from Weston, and it's ruined!" Pargeter's second rushed to his side, just as he tumbled down on the grass in a dead faint.

"Idiot," muttered Psyche, as their coach began to move.

Aimee gazed down at Kenneth leaning against her, and she put her arms around him. The shadows beneath his eyes looked even more pronounced than they had been, now that his face was so pale, and he looked thin, his skin stretched over his cheekbones, his nose, and chin. He breathed as if he were asleep, and she prayed that this was all it was, sleep, and not anything worse. She pushed back a lock of hair from his forehead, and did not care if anyone saw her kiss him gently there. Her heart ached, and she knew she would love him, no matter what. Even if he were foolish, and stubborn, even if he had been unfaithful to her. Later, she would find out the truth about Miss Rivers, and make her decision whether to leave him.

She wished she loved him less; then she could keep to her betrothal and look the other way if he were truly unfaithful. But she loved him with all her heart, and knew she could not. It would tear her apart; better that she break the betrothal, and go back to her uncle's house, and never hear from him again.

But she knew nothing yet. Nothing to base any decision on. First Kenneth must become well. Then, then she would decide.

It was impossible to keep Kenneth's condition from Lady Hathaway, of course. It was well after dawn when they entered the Hathaway house, and Trimble's face neglected to become wooden first and went straight to being alarmed. It was useless to suppose the butler would keep the news to himself, and more than one maid had seen Harry and a stout footman carry Kenneth up to his room.

It was all Psyche could do to calm her mother when the news came to her, and Lady Hathaway was only a little assuaged when the doctor said that Kenneth had suffered only a little graze to the head, and not even a fracture that he could see. But the captain, he said, was in a state of exhaustion—he had seen many soldiers in this condition when they came back from battle—and though the wound would heal in a matter of a few weeks, he highly recommended rest and bland foods. At least two months' worth of rest in the country would be best.

"As for Miss Rivers . . ." The doctor looked uncomfortably at Lady Hathaway who was sitting in the drawing room, wringing her hands, then went on hurriedly. "She is exhausted as well, and, ahem, is probably expecting an Interesting Event in about five or six months."

"Oh, heavens!" Lady Hathaway said, and cast a quick, anxious glance at Aimee.

Aimee's hands curled into fists in her lap, and her stomach burned with nausea. There was some other explanation, of course. Kenneth was known to be a kind man . . . perhaps he had offered to help this young woman in her distress. Perhaps he had nothing to do with her . . . condition. She took in a deep breath.

"Perhaps it would be well if all of us retired to the countryside," she said, glad her voice was not shaking as she herself was. "I confess I am quite fatigued myself by all the activities we have gone to of late. I know Psyche will not object, and certainly Kenneth and . . . Miss Rivers would be better for it."

Lady Hathaway pulled at the handkerchief in her hand in a distracted manner. "If you think—But I do not know—Oh, heavens! I am sure all of us would be better off at our home near Tunbridge Wells, and if anyone wished, they could partake of the waters there." She rose and paced in an agitated manner. "If only Sir John had not gone to Edinburgh! But there is no help for it—I must write him a letter, letting him know what has come about." She turned to the doctor and smiled slightly. "I thank you, Doctor Kent. I do appreciate your services." The doctor bowed and left, and Lady Hathaway rang for the butler.

"Trimble," she said when he arrived. "Do prepare for

our departure back home. My son needs the fresh country air to recover, and I wish to go immediately."

"Yes, my lady," Trimble said, a look of relief on his face.

Aimee gazed out the window at the sky, quite bright now with the noon sun, shining as if nothing untoward had happened this morning. It seemed almost as if it were a horrible dream . . . but of course it was not, and it was quite real, for here they were, going to leave London for the Hathaways' home in the country. More waiting. She would have to wait a little longer for the answers—she could not ask Kenneth or Miss Rivers now. She would have to wait until they got to Tunbridge Wells.

They took two coaches, the Hathaways' and a hired one for the journey, since they had to carry two invalids. The coaches were piled high with luggage without, and the family squeezed themselves in one carriage, with Miss Rivers and some servants in the other.

The sun shone throughout their journey, and the weather was thankfully clear, though Aimee felt that clouds and rain would be more suited to her mood than blue sky. She had little conversation, and could not think of anything to say to Kenneth unless it was full of hurtful questions. But she did manage to smile from time to time, and that was, thankfully, enough, for Kenneth did not speak much either; he gazed at her often when he was awake, and spoke little. But mostly he slept.

It would have been idyllic, Kenneth thought, if he had not been so tired. As the buildings of London disappeared through the window and wide expanses of bright blue sky and green fields showed through the carriage window instead, he felt a lifting of spirits and his body ached with a good ache that told him it had released the tension and was relaxing at last.

He did not say any of this to Aimee in the coach. His

head still ached from the bullet graze, he was still bone-tired, and his mouth did not seem to want to work very often to form the words he thought. And his mother and Psyche were there in the coach, fussing over him, and he wished to talk to Aimee in private.

He drifted in and out of sleep, and felt content to gaze at his betrothed. He had been a fool, he knew. He smiled slightly. Perhaps it was a good thing that he had received that wound to his head. It had knocked some sense into him. He knew it as soon as he had opened his eyes and seen Aimee's frightened and tearstained face above him as he lay on the ground at Hyde Park. Dizzy as he'd been, he'd looked at her face and knew he'd been confused, that his love for her was deep and sure, so much so that he felt he'd been shot to the heart looking at her sweet face and anxious eyes. How could he have doubted his love? He would tell her of it and everything he had meant to tell her while he was away at war as soon as he was well, as soon as he stopped being tired. There would be no misunderstanding this time, not like all the times before when he had snapped at her—out of fatigue, he knew that now.

The green fields and trees became more familiar, and when they passed Tunbridge Wells to the countryside beyond, he smiled. This was what he remembered those long hot days in the Spanish sun—the cool green fields and hills of his home. He had dreamed of this, had yearned for it as he had yearned for Aimee. He'd been doubly a fool not to have come here immediately, for he knew his superior officer would have given him enough furlough to do as he wished. But instead he'd felt duty bound to stay at headquarters working, and then there was the problem of crippled and out-of-work veterans that sorely needed attention.

He hadn't thought, of course. If General Marsdon was

more than willing to allow him furlough, then he needn't have stayed at headquarters. And writing letters about veterans could easily have been done here at home. Something in him had kept pushing at him to go and go and go, and he could not stop working somehow.

The carriage finally stopped, and though he insisted on walking into the house, dizziness almost overcame him and he was frankly glad of the stout arm of Jackson, his valet, to support him so that he did not fall and humiliate himself. At last he was undressed, and he sank into the soft down mattress of his bed, and slept.

Aimee took it upon herself to attend to both Kenneth and Miss Rivers—she was good at nursing, and it forced her to be as impartial as possible. She could not assume that Miss Rivers's child was Kenneth's. The young woman had said nothing about it, and had only asked to speak to him. Somehow the fact that she tended Miss Rivers made her think more clearly—it was nonsensical, of course, but she felt that if she nursed her that Miss Rivers could not repay her with wrong. It did not matter. She felt she must do something to keep herself calm.

Psyche also took care of them both, and Aimee could see she was subdued, no doubt because she was concerned about her brother.

A sound came from the bed, and Aimee turned to look at Miss Rivers, whose eyes fluttered and opened. She drew in a deep breath. "I must be dreaming," she said slowly.

Aimee smiled at her. "No, you are not. You are at the Hathaways' estate, not far from Tunbridge Wells. You became ill when you came to call on us in London, and when we came home, we took you with us, for we could not leave you behind."

The girl's lower lip trembled. "You are very kind. But I cannot stay. I must find Lieutenant Hathaway."

A sharp pang went through Aimee's heart, but she managed another smile at Miss Rivers. "Captain Hathaway is here in this house, recovering from a wound. When both of you are well, you may speak to him."

The girl gasped and sat up. "A wound? Oh, dear God. How bad is it? Will he live?" She seized Aimee's arm. "Please, I must go to him!"

Aimee felt as if ice were forming around her heart, and she forced herself to smile again. "He is not badly wounded at all," she replied steadily. "He is mostly fatigued, and indeed has been up and about."

Miss Rivers breathed a sigh of relief. "Has . . . has he asked about me at all?" she asked.

"I am afraid he does not know you are here yet," Aimee said, as kindly as she could.

A woebegone expression crossed Miss Rivers's face. "I . . . I would have thought he might have mentioned me. We are betrothed, after all."

Aimee rose abruptly and stepped away from the girl, feeling ill.

"Is there anything wrong, Miss Mattingly?" the girl asked anxiously.

Everything was wrong. Aimee wanted to scream her anguish, but she could not, and breathed deeply instead. "No . . . no, of course not. I seem suddenly to have the headache. If you will excuse me, I will call Miss Hathaway to attend you."

She rushed out the room. She could not wait any longer, she'd felt sick with speculation and was now sick with the realization that Kenneth had lied to her, had lain with this Miss Rivers, and got a child on her, probably promising her marriage. She could not understand it; she never would have thought Kenneth would be so lost to honor.

She had to go to her own home, to her uncle's house. Quickly, she ran to her chambers and rang for a maid. She had some bandboxes under her bed—she pulled them out and began stuffing her clothes into them, randomly and without thought to whether they would crease or not. She seized the jewelry box that sat on the dressing table and threw it in a bandbox as well, hearing the necklaces and earrings clash against each other as they spilled out of it. Tears fell from her cheeks and she dashed them away. She would not cry, no, she would not! He was not worth it, the odious, faithless monster. Quickly she wrote a note to Lady Hathaway—she could not leave without explanation—and left it on her dressing table.

She ordered a carriage and as she went down the stairs she spied a scullery maid. Of course she could not go without a maid, and she hurriedly pulled a few shillings out from her reticule and pressed them into the maid's hands, asking her to come with her. The maid readily agreed, and within a few minutes, they were on the road to her uncle's house near Cambridge.

The tears rose in Aimee's throat again as she looked out the window and saw the Hathaways' country house grow smaller and smaller. She could not cry, even now, not with the maid to see her. She would have to wait until she arrived in Cambridge, and then she would go to her old room, the one she had wept in when she had first arrived at her uncle's, not long after her parents had died.

Aimee stared out at the countryside, concentrating on the trees and the buildings that passed, and soon she succeeded in stemming the tears that threatened to spill again and again. As the miles stretched between her and Kenneth, she began to feel as if her heart grew colder and colder, as if she had encased it in ice and had become numb with cold.

It was just as well. If she allowed herself to feel anything, she would break apart inside. And she could not, not until she returned home.

# Chapter 10

When a maid came to Psyche in the music room with the message that Miss Mattingly wished her to come to attend Miss Rivers, Psyche rose slowly and went up the stairs just as slowly. It was not that she was reluctant to attend Miss Rivers. It was just that since their move back home, she had not seen Harry, and she was certain he was angry at her. Well, she was angry at him, too, for that matter. But though they always made up afterward, she hated the period before the making up. She always felt so low, for even when she was angry, she still liked to have her best friend about to talk to. She shrugged. Perhaps he was looking for that person he had mentioned before. He said he'd been looking for her for a long time. She'd wondered who she was, but had never got around to asking, for there was always something more amusing to think about or do when Harry was around.

Miss Rivers was sitting up in bed when Psyche knocked and entered, and she was glad of that. The poor girl had looked quite pale and worn, but now she looked much better. Her face, however, was clearly worried.

"Is there something the matter?" Psyche asked.

Miss Rivers bit her lip. "I . . . I am afraid I might have said something to upset Miss Mattingly—she rushed out of the room so quickly, and had turned so pale." A tear fell down the girl's cheek. "I would not want to upset her for the world—she has been so kind, indeed all of you have!"

"Miss Mattingly has been under a bit of a strain lately," Psyche said, and patted the girl's hand comfortingly. "Whatever did you say to her?"

"Nothing that might upset anyone, I am sure," Miss Rivers said, and shook her head. "I merely asked to speak to Lieut—that is, Captain Hathaway, and wondered if he might have spoken of me to her, or to anyone."

"No, I am afraid he has not mentioned you to me at least, and I am sure he would have—I am his sister, you know," Psyche said kindly.

Another tear fell down the girl's cheek, and her woe-begone expression increased. "I thought . . . I thought he might have mentioned me to his relatives. We are be-trothed, you see."

The room took a quick spin around Psyche, and she took in a deep breath to steady herself. "What . . . what did you say?"

"I . . . I am betrothed to him," Miss Rivers said, and looked frightened. "I . . . I suppose he did not tell you."

"No . . . no, he did not." Psyche clasped her hands to-gether tightly in her lap. "I—Do you think you might be well enough to dress and come with me?" She forced her-self to smile at the girl. "You need not be afraid. I am not angry at you. I think a few things need to be made . . . more clear than they are now."

"Yes," Miss Rivers replied. "I am feeling much better now, and I do think I need not stay in bed any longer."

"Good." Psyche rose from the side of the bed. "I need to find Miss Mattingly, and then I will come back to you."

But Aimee was nowhere to be found. Psyche went to her room and found the note, hastily scrawled and blurred with teardrops, so that it was difficult to read. It was clear, however, that she had left and gone home. An angry fire burned in Psyche, and she could feel her temper rising. She could not blame Aimee for leaving. Kenneth had acted in a most strange and inconsistent way throughout their stay in London, and now . . . and now it seemed he had been unfaithful to her, and had ruined Miss Rivers as well. She rang for a servant, and when a maid appeared, bade her give Aimee's note to Lady Hathaway.

Miss Rivers was dressed in a borrowed morning dress by the time Psyche returned to her room. She smiled at her reassuringly. "Do come with me, Miss Rivers. I think it is about time you spoke with my brother."

Kenneth sat in the large conservatory just outside of the house and felt the sun streaming down upon him through the large windows. If he closed his eyes, he could imagine he was in the middle of an English summer instead of spring, the air heavy with warm moisture and the scent of earth as if it had just finished raining. He was feeling much better—he had been a fool indeed, not leaving for home earlier. He had slept more than he ever had before, going to bed not long after sunset and arising not much before noon. He had walked through the fields and the woods, a little at first, and then a little longer, and the fresh cool air that flowed into his lungs seemed to spread into his blood and made him feel as if he had been newly washed inside and out. When next he saw Aimee, he would ask that she go with him on his walks, and it would be like it was before he had gone to war. They would hold each other's hands, twining their fingers together as they walked, and when they were far enough away from the house, he would kiss her breathless, until she moaned and pressed herself against him in that sudden passionate way she had.

He sighed and rose from his chair. Perhaps he would go seek her now. It was still early in the afternoon.

Footsteps made him turn quickly, and he spied Psyche coming toward him, a grim look on her face. A pretty young lady walked behind her, possibly some neighbor, for she looked vaguely familiar. He grinned at his sister.

"What has upset you, Psyche? You look as if you wanted to rip something apart."

"Yes," Psyche said, and stared at him angrily. "You."

Kenneth laughed. "I? What have I done?"

She stepped aside and brought the young lady forward. "Kenneth, may I present Miss Mary Rivers. Miss Rivers, may I present Captain Kenneth Hathaway."

He bowed over the lady's hand. "I am pleased to meet you." He transferred his gaze to Psyche, meeting her puzzled eyes. "Is there something amiss?" A small moan brought his attention back to Miss Rivers.

"But . . . but you are not Francis!" the girl faltered. "I thought . . . I thought you were Lieutenant Francis Pargeter-Hathaway."

"Francis *Pargeter*," Kenneth said automatically.

"Not Pargeter-Hathaway," Psyche said, and suddenly sat down on the chair that Kenneth had vacated. "Oh, dear." She covered her mouth with her hands and closed her eyes.

Kenneth stared at Miss Rivers, trying to recall where he had seen her last—not a neighbor, perhaps, but . . .

"Salamanca," he said, and frowned, trying to remember the details. "You were there—I think we found some French brandy."

Miss Rivers blushed and nodded. "Yes. I would not blame you if you thought me like . . . like those women who went with the other men. But I remember you now, you were very kind." She turned to Psyche, biting her lower lip, and brushed away a tear. "My father was the surgeon, and he . . . he died of a fever directly after the battle. I had nowhere to go, and I didn't know what to do. Your brother was very kind and gave me some money, and then Francis—Lieutenant Pargeter—he took me in and . . ." She blushed even more red than before, and her hand went to her belly in a protective gesture. She looked away from them. "He promised to marry me."

Psyche eyed her brother. "Is that what Mr. D'Amant meant when he said you 'hath a way' with the—"

"No!" Kenneth said hastily. "I never did! Though what the devil Harry thought he was doing telling my sister such things—But never mind that!" He looked at Miss Rivers apologetically. "I remember now—you reminded me a bit of Aimee, when she had lost her parents . . . and I'm afraid I might be a bit at fault. Not that way!" he exclaimed when Psyche shot him a reproachful look. "I had celebrated a bit much with the French brandy—and I don't know how it came about, but Miss Rivers here seemed to have wandered into my tent during the night."

"I did not!" Miss Rivers cried. "I remember I had gone with Francis, and woke up there, too."

"That's because I put you there," Kenneth said. "Couldn't have you in my tent that morning and the word get to Aimee somehow. I hadn't done anything, after all! I remembered you had gone with Pargeter, and thought maybe that's where you were staying." He grimaced. "Thing is, I wasn't thinking very clearly. Not after a bottle of brandy in me. I was as sick as a dog, too."

"But what am I to do?" Miss Rivers cried, wringing her hands. "I need to find Francis!"

Psyche and Kenneth exchanged a long look, and then Kenneth let out a long breath. "Well, I think it would be best if you stayed here for now. I'll see what I can do about finding the lieutenant for you."

"Kenneth is right, Miss Rivers," Psyche said. "The

best thing would be if you went back to your room and
rested a little—you look quite pale, and I am sure you
have suffered a severe shock, finding out that my brother
is not your—your betrothed." She waved both hands at
her in a shooing motion. "Do go—you know your way,
do you not?"

Miss Rivers looked at them, her expression a little
more hopeful, and nodded. "You are quite right, Miss
Hathaway," she said. "I think . . . I think I will write a letter to him, and if the captain would be so kind as to de-
liver it to him when he finds him, I would be very
grateful."

"Of course," Kenneth said, and smiled kindly at her.

It took a few minutes of Miss Rivers's exclamations of
undying gratitude before Kenneth and Psyche were left
alone at last.

"Poor Miss Rivers!" Psyche said. "She cannot know
what a horrid person Pargeter is! I think he was trying to
snatch Aimee out from under your nose, Kenneth, and
that only from spite, all the while he was betrothed to
Miss Rivers."

"I'm sure of it, damn his eyes," Kenneth said, and
frowned. "Poor little thing! The chit seemed rather taken
with the brute. I can't think she'd be happy with him." He
sighed. "Well, it's not really any affair of ours—I'm
happy enough to find the man for her, and then it's up to
them. Thank goodness Aimee didn't hear of any of this—
What was that?"

"She *did* hear of it," Psyche said, a little louder, and
pulled a leaf from a fern, obviously not wanting to meet
his eyes. "That's why she's not here right now."

"*What*?!"

"She went home to her uncle's house. She thought—
well, Miss Rivers said that she was betrothed to you—

Lieutenant Hathaway, that is, and the doctor said that she was increasing, so of course Aimee thought—"

"Damn and *blast*!" Kenneth roared. "Why didn't you tell me as soon as you came here?" Swiftly he strode to the conservatory door and thrust it open, Psyche hurrying after him.

"Well, I couldn't help thinking the same thing! And I could hardly blame Aimee for leaving since it seemed you were the cause of poor Miss Rivers's ruin!"

"How could you think—Devil take it, Psyche! I'm your brother! You *know* me! I would never do such a thing."

"Well, how should I know?" Psyche said tartly. "You were always very wild when you were in school, and then Bertie Garthwaite once said you were in the petticoat line, which made me think he must have meant you liked being with ladies more than most, because I could not conceive of you selling ladies' clothing at a draper's—we Hathaways have never been in trade, after all!"

"What in the world—trade? Drapers?" Kenneth gave her a scornful look. "If I didn't know you for a rattletrap, Psyche, I'd think you were mad going on about such things when I'm trying to fix a mess of your making." The stables loomed ahead and he hastened his steps. "Jack!" he called. "Get me a horse—Flasher's the best— and saddle him." A young boy stumbled out of one of the stalls and nodded, hastily running off for the horse.

"Mess of my—! I did not make this mess!" Psyche protested. "I had nothing to do with Aimee leaving!"

"Well, if you had told me Aimee had left earlier this morning, I would have caught up with her by now." The stable boy had brought a strong bay horse, and after testing the girths, Kenneth mounted it.

"Of all the odious, unjust—!"

"Never mind that!" Kenneth said. "Tell Mother where

I have gone and why." He grinned at her. "I know I can depend on you to tell her the whole." The bay tossed its head and stamped its feet, reflecting the restless impatience Kenneth felt, and he let loose the reins at last.

Psyche watched her brother ride off and shook her head. She wished he had waited, and perhaps brought her with him as well as Miss Rivers. She was not at all sure, after all that had gone on between Kenneth and his betrothed, that Aimee would believe him. Even now he acted wildly, and she had no idea whether Harry had reversed the love arrow's effect on Kenneth or not. He had had the opportunity . . . but Harry had grown angry at her and had left before telling her.

There was really nothing for it, then. She had no choice but to bring Miss Rivers to Squire Garthwaite's house, and hope that Aimee had not refused to see Kenneth when he arrived. Even if she had, perhaps she would listen to Psyche and certainly to Miss Rivers. Psyche pressed her lips together. She did not need Harry to make things better between Kenneth and Aimee, after all. She could very well do it herself!

It was almost night when Aimee arrived at her uncle's estate near Cambridge. She could not easily see it in the gloom, but she knew the ivy-covered stone was the same, and the shapes of the old oak and alder near the road to the house were dearly familiar. She swallowed and dabbed at a tear with her gloved hand. She would show a face as cheerful as possible to her dear uncle Joseph and all would be as it was before she had left for Lady Hathaway's patronage and her Season in London.

A foolish effort, to be sure! For when Aimee entered her uncle's study and saw his burly form comfortably ensconced in his chair by the fire and reading a book, she could not help bursting into tears. Immediately she was enfolded in big bearlike arms, and patted on her back.

"My dear niece, what is this?" He drew her to a chair opposite his and squeezed her hand kindly. "Are you ill? Where is Lady Hathaway? Is she with you?"

For a moment Aimee could do nothing but shake her head, but finally she wiped the tears from her eyes and blew her nose with the large handkerchief her uncle had given her. He waited patiently, looking at her over his spectacles in kind concern.

"It's Kenneth, Uncle Joseph. He is—he is a monster!"

Squire Garthwaite raised his eyebrows. "The last time I saw him, Aimee-girl, he looked quite normal to me. Rather like a young man in love, the way he was looking at you."

Tears threatened to burst from her again, but she swallowed hard and shook her head. "No, no, he is not, not anymore. He is betrothed to another, and she—she is with child and he never told me, no, not the whole time we were in London. He *pretended* to love me, but he never said it, and so I knew there was something wrong, and there was!"

The squire rocked back in his chair and blew out a long breath. "Now that's a sorry tale and one I never thought to hear about young Hathaway, I can tell you. But . . . are you sure?"

Aimee nodded, and related the whole. The squire was silent while she talked, his face growing more thoughtful as she went on. Finally, she was finished, and he nodded.

"It looks very bad, very bad indeed," he said, and she looked at him with quick indignation at his mild tone of voice. He held up a hand. "And it's not that I don't believe you—I do. But he's my son's friend also, and I've never known Bertie to take up with a rogue or any other bad 'un. I'm thinking there's another tail to this dog of a

story that's not being told, and it'd be a good thing for
you to think on it for a bit, for sure as I'm the squire, the
young captain's going to come for you."

Aimee shook her head. "I . . . I don't think I will wish
to see him if he comes here."

"Do as you wish on that head," her uncle said, and patted her hand again. "But he'll be here, if I know that boy."
He rose and pulled the bell rope. "Meanwhile, I think you
should go up to your room—I'll wager you're tired, my
girl, and need your rest. Or, if you wish to listen to a rat-
tle, Bertie's here—heard I had caught myself a fine tom
pheasant and he was hoping to try out the new cook's
ragout." Aimee smiled at him and gave him a quick kiss
on the cheek before she left with the maid to her room.

The squire sat silently in his study for a moment, purs-
ing his lips in thought. Then he pulled the bell rope again.
"Barton," he said, when the butler arrived. "When Captain Hathaway comes to the house—and I expect he'll be
here this evening—don't admit him right away. Let him
cool his heels for a moment. And if you see him scaling
the walls of the house or breaking into any of the rooms
from a window, neither you nor any of the other servants
are to stop him, do you hear?"

The butler only raised his eyebrows for a moment before bowing in assent. Squire Garthwaite smiled wryly.
"There's nothing like a nice climb into a window to convince a girl she's wanted, eh, Barton? I daresay that Miss
Rivers is looking to snatch a man by showing her belly,
but I think I know young Hathaway well enough to know
he's not the sort to sow without reaping his due. It's all
nonsense, I'll wager."

"As you say, sir," Barton replied, and left the study.

Captain Hathaway was not in a good mood by the time he
reached Squire Garthwaite's house. His horse had thrown

a shoe halfway to his destination, and he had to find a blacksmith to fix it. He'd been hoping to catch up to Aimee on the road, but he never would now, for the blacksmith had to be called from a wedding feast and had been reluctant to do the job. And if Aimee had told her uncle what had caused her to leave his mother's protection, he'd have to contend with the squire first, and he had no wish to come to fisticuffs with his friend's father.

It was quite dark now, and as he dismounted from his horse and walked up the steps to Garthwaite Manor, he took in a deep breath and let it out again. He might as well get on with it. He took the brass knocker in hand and gave it a sharp rap.

The door opened immediately and the squire's dour butler bowed but did not make room for Kenneth to enter. "May I say who is calling, sir?" he said.

Kenneth's ire rose. He did not need this sort of insolence when he'd had a trying day of it so far. "Damn you, Barton, you know very well who I am, and I daresay I'm expected, too!" he said. "Kenneth Hathaway, come to call on Miss Aimee Mattingly, my betrothed. And don't say she isn't here, because I know she is."

"Yes, sir," Barton said. "But I have been instructed not to admit you."

"By whom? Aimee?"

"By Squire Garthwaite, sir. I'm very sorry, sir." The door closed.

A fire of anger burned hot and fast through Kenneth, and burst out in a series of blistering curses in both English and Spanish. But the door in front of him was unresponsive, and he was still left out in the cold night air. His anger burned higher and made him pace restlessly in front of the mansion. He *would* get in, damn it—he had to talk to Aimee, and explain everything. He could not let her end this day thinking he was the worst kind of mon-

ster, the kind who would betray every oath he gave to another, especially to the woman he loved. He could imagine the hurt she must have felt, and cursed again, but
without much heat, for his anger suddenly faded, thinking of Aimee weeping. No, he could not let her go to bed,
no doubt brokenhearted, before he talked to her.

He remembered, long ago, when he used to call upon
her here that she had a room above the drawing room,
looking out at the field in the back of the mansion, and
that a huge trellis was secured next her window so as to
support some roses that had been planted there. He had
climbed it before to steal a kiss from her a few
evenings—he could climb it again he was sure.

Swiftly he strode around the house—yes, there it was,
the trellis growing quite high with climbing roses just beginning to bud. It had been years since he'd done this,
and the rosebush was no longer a small bush, but had
crawled up the side of the house almost over the window.
He grasped one stake of the trellis.

"Damn!" He'd grabbed a rose stem, too, and the thorns
had gone right through his gloves. He looked up at
Aimee's window and gritted his teeth. Very well! Thorns
or no thorns, he would climb the damned trellis, and if he
were a bleeding shredded corpse by the time he reached
the top, so be it.

A light tap-tapping woke Aimee from her uneasy sleep
into which she had fallen after another bout of weeping.
She sat up and looked about her, bewildered, at the room
dimly revealed by a brace of candles she had lit earlier,
until she remembered that she had returned to her uncle
Joseph's house.

*Tap-tap!* The sound was coming from outside. Aimee
pulled on her dressing gown and cautiously looked out of

the window. Suddenly a face appeared in it, and she drew back with a little scream.

"It's I, Aimee! Let me in!"

Kenneth! A flicker of anger burned in her and she shook her head.

"Dash it all, I almost fell twice climbing up here, and I swear I'm nearly shredded to threads from the thorns—let me in!"

"No, you—you libertine!" Aimee said. "Go away."

Kenneth's forehead thumped on the window and she could hear a frustrated groan. "I am not a libertine. I am *not* a libertine. I haven't been so lucky as to be even *close* to being one in more than four years," he said, thumping his head on the window on the last three words. "Let me in and I can explain everything, I swear it."

"I think Miss Rivers explained it clearly enough," Aimee said.

There was a sharp crack and for one moment Kenneth's face disappeared with much rustling and what sounded very close to "damned bloody trellis," coming from a short distance below the window. More rustling ensued, and Kenneth appeared again, looking grim.

"Let me in, Aimee, *please*, or I swear I'll break the window."

"No. It is quite improper for you to come into my room this way—in any way. And especially not if you are going to use such language in my presence."

"I swear—I promise I won't." His voice sounded almost wheedling; Aimee could not remember Kenneth wheedling since before he had gone off to war. She hesitated. He sounded different—irritated, to be sure, but without the tense undercurrent she had heard since he had come home. "Aimee, please. It wasn't I. It was Pargeter—you know the way he has of calling himself Pargeter-Hathaway. And it isn't *that* improper if I come in—no one has seen me up here, and we are betrothed, after all."

Her uncle had said there might be another side to this story. . . . Aimee bit her lip, then stepped forward and opened the window.

"Thank God," Kenneth said, and pulled himself up over the windowsill and fell over onto the floor. "I don't know why it seemed much easier to climb four years ago. Either I'm getting heavier or that's a devilishly made trellis."

Aimee pressed her lips together firmly to suppress a sudden giggle. "I think you've grown since then," she said.

"No doubt," he said, and grinned at her in the old way he used to, so that her heart tightened painfully. He pushed back a lock of hair on his forehead with his hand and something dark smeared his brow.

"Oh! Oh, dear, I think you are bleeding." She rushed forward and took his hand, and pulled him toward the candles next to her bed. A cut scored his palm and blood oozed slowly from it. She made him sit on the bed, then found a cloth and dipped it into a washbowl in which she had poured some water from a pitcher. She glanced at him, and found him watching her. Her hand stopped just over his palm for a moment, and then she swallowed and looked away, concentrating on wiping the blood from his hand and then the smear from his forehead.

Finally, she put down the cloth, crossing her arms in front of her. "Well, now that you are cleaned up, you may give me your explanation."

Kenneth stared at her for a moment, as if he was not sure where to begin. "I won't say I've never seen Miss Rivers before, because I have and that was in Spain. She'd lost her father, and she was grief stricken—reminded me of you, the first day I saw you. I felt dashed sorry for her, so I gave her some money to pay her way back to England and that was the end of it, I thought, since she went off with Pargeter."

He hesitated, then continued. "We celebrated one evening after a battle, and I drank too much brandy and was sick as a dog the next day, and there she was in my tent the next morning."

Aimee closed her eyes and turned away, but Kenneth grasped her shoulders and turned her toward him. "But I didn't do anything but return her to Pargeter's tent, and that's the truth of it." He shook her a little. "Look at me, Aimee. I've told you the whole truth, even though I didn't have to tell you all of it. I wouldn't want someone coming to you later telling you what I'd left out, because then you'd think me a liar. And I'm not that, Aimee. I am not *that*—and you know it, for I've never lied to you."

She looked at him at last, and saw that the shadows beneath his eyes had lessened. "No, you are not a liar, Kenneth. I know it. But you would not tell me—you seemed so distant when you came back, and for all that you said you worshiped me, you never said you loved me."

He gave a low groan and pulled her to him, resting his forehead on her shoulder. "I'm a fool, Aimee. You don't know—I was so tired. Sometimes I felt I could not continue fighting, and there were times I'd lost hope, but I dared not let anyone see it. I couldn't let my men down, couldn't let them see I was afraid or felt too tired to go on."

Aimee leaned her cheek against his hair and tentatively stroked it with her hand, the chill ice around her heart slowly melting into tears.

"But I had to keep moving and keep rallying them on, even though I knew half of them would die," he said, and his hold on her tightened. "I couldn't rest. But I had your portrait, and I'd look at it, and remember you and that was what made me go on, the hope that I'd see you again." He gave a hesitant laugh. "That was all I had, that and your letters and the letters from my family. And then I began to forget what my family looked like after so long and after so much blood and death. But I could look at your portrait, and that was when I remembered England and everything I fought for. I think . . . I think you became something other than my own Aimee after that—a goal, a prize, a goddess. Not quite real."

He raised his head and cupped her face between his hands, looking at her as if he were memorizing each feature. "Then I came home, and nothing was as I remembered it. Psyche had grown, and the cobblestones of London were nothing like the green fields in my imagination. Even you had changed—or rather, you were real instead of the distant marble goddess I'd made up in my mind." He shook his head. "You'll think me an idiot, I know—but I couldn't stop thinking of you as the girl in the portrait, not the girl I'd known before I left England for Spain. It was as if once I'd made up my mind to keep fighting, I couldn't stop."

"Oh, Kenneth!" Aimee took his hand and squeezed it tightly. "I wish you had told me. I did not understand—and you acted so strangely. And then when Miss Rivers came, I thought she was the reason you did not wish to kiss me."

"It was the dam—dashed portrait. Every time I looked at it, I couldn't think of doing anything but dashed near worshiping it. When I lost it—but I did find it again, Aimee—I think I started looking at you more and remembering . . ."

Aimee stared at him, her heart thumping wildly, for he was looking at her with a hungry expression. "Remembering what?" she whispered.

"Remembering what it was like to kiss you," he said, and put his lips upon hers.

With a sob, she put her arms around him, leaning into his kiss, opening her mouth under his. This was her Kenneth, the one who had left so long ago, and he was truly home now. She knew it by the way he moved his lips over her mouth and her cheek to her throat, the way he slid his hand down to her waist and pulled her closer to him. "I've missed you, Kenneth. I've missed you so horribly." The tears she had held back flowed over at last.

"Don't cry, Aimee, love," he murmured, kissing her cheek, and then his lips were on hers again, and she could taste the salt of her own tears upon them. He pressed her back, and she felt the bed behind her, then tumbled upon it. He laughed, a shaken sound, and kissed her again, pulling at the strings of her dressing gown. She did not care that there was then only her shift between them or that he pushed aside one shoulder of her gown so that he could kiss the skin he exposed. She had missed him so terribly, and she felt as if she wanted to take him into herself somehow, so that he would never leave her. A shimmering heat rose up from her belly as he kissed and touched her, and she moved under him to bring him closer.

Suddenly he gasped and rolled away from her. "Not until we are married," he said. He drew in a deep breath and let it out again. "You are right. It is damned improper for me to be in your room this way." He looked toward the window and grimaced. "I suppose I should go out the way I came in and try the front door again. Do you think you could tell Barton to let me in?"

Aimee sighed. "Yes, of course." She glanced shyly at him. "Do we really need to wait until we are married?"

Kenneth pulled her to him and kissed her again. "Yes, devil take it," he said. "If I know my mother, she'll want a big wedding for us and it'll take months to plan. Wouldn't want anything havey-cavey about the arrival of our first child, you know."

Aimee blushed and laid her head on his chest. "I suppose not." She pushed him away. "Go, then, and I'll see you downstairs."

"Right you are." Kenneth moved toward the window, then stopped. He put his hand inside his pocket and drew out an oval object. He gazed at it for a long moment, then frowned. Suddenly he threw it into the fireplace into the fire.

"What are you doing? Is that not my portrait?" Aimee asked.

Kenneth smiled at her. "I don't need it, love. I have the real woman I love—I don't need a portrait to remind me of that." He strode to the window and put his leg over the windowsill. He gave a last long look at her and smiled. "I love you, Aimee," he said, and swung himself around and onto the rose trellis. She heard another sharp crack and winced when she heard muffled curses, rustling, and a thump below. But when she looked out the window, he only smiled and waved at her before he walked around the corner of the house. With a sigh, she took off her dressing gown, pulled out a dress from her wardrobe, and prepared herself to go downstairs.

Psyche swore that if she ever helped Kenneth again, she would exact payment from him to the fullest degree. For all that she felt sorry for Miss Rivers and wished desperately to help her brother and Aimee, it was not pleasant to be in a rocking carriage with a lady who was with child and moaned that she felt ill at every bump and curve in the road. But family was family, after all, and she had always been taught that one did what one must when it came to furthering the interests of loved ones. However, no one said that one should not be recompensed for it, especially if it were for the sake of an ungrateful brother!

The carriage stopped at last, and Psyche opened the door with relief and helped the still-moaning Miss Rivers down from it. A horse was standing in front of the house—she recognized Flasher at once, and knew that Kenneth was already here. She hoped that he was speaking with Aimee already; perhaps it would be enough to wait until they were done to present Miss Rivers to tell her story as well. She went up the steps to the door and knocked.

"Please tell Squire Garthwaite that Miss Psyche Hathaway and Miss Rivers are here to see him, please," Psyche said when the butler opened the door. The butler seemed to choke, but recovered, and bowed, opening the door wider for her to step in. It was not long before she was ushered into the presence of the squire. She had never met him, but liked him immediately, for he was a big comfortable bear of a man, and his eyes twinkled merrily at her.

"And what can I do for you ladies?" he said, after she and Miss Rivers curtsied.

"Please, sir, I understand my brother is here and perhaps speaking with Aimee."

The squire frowned for a moment. "Probably not yet. I believe he is climbing the rose trellis to her room right now."

Psyche stared at him. "The rose trellis . . . ?"

He nodded. "Yes. Nothing like a good bit of exercise to work off one's bad humor. He'll have used up all the curses he learned in his life by the time he reaches the top, I'm sure."

Psyche burst into laughter. "Oh, heavens! I can just see it, too." She wiped her eyes with her fingers and sat on the chair he indicated when she had entered.

The squire smiled at her. "Now, what can I do for you?"

"I was thinking perhaps we should go up to Aimee and have Miss Rivers tell her that she is very mistaken about Kenneth. Because, you see, Miss Rivers is not betrothed to Kenneth, but to Francis Pargeter, who has a habit of calling himself Pargeter-Hathaway because he is a distant cousin of ours, and of course she thought he was Kenneth."

"It's true," Miss Rivers chimed in. "And I could not wish that poor Miss Mattingly think that her betrothed played her false, although . . ." She began to cry. "Although I am afraid that it is Francis Pargeter who played me false, alas!"

Psyche restrained herself from doing something so unfeeling as grimace, and patted Miss Rivers's hand and gave her a handkerchief instead. "It shall come about, you shall see. If Mr. Pargeter cannot be made to come up to scratch, then we shall see what we can do to provide for you," Psyche said, wantonly committing her family's resources to Miss Rivers's aid.

"But I love him!" Miss Rivers cried. Psyche cast a helpless look at Squire Garthwaite who grimaced and gave her a sympathetic glance.

"Now see here, young lady," he said. "No one is going to throw you out into the snow, so there's no need to act like a Tragedy Jill. We can always—"

The door opened and Bertie Garthwaite came in. "Father, that new cook of yours is not as good as he should be. The pheasant he made up into a ragout did not sit well with me at all. Better to get a French cook or perhaps Italian—" He stopped, caught sight of Psyche and Miss Rivers's tear-streaked face, winced, and began to sidle toward the door like a startled crab. "Er, sorry. Didn't know you had guests."

"Do come in and pay your respects, my boy," the squire said quickly, obviously taking advantage of the interruption.

Miss Rivers hastily dabbed her cheeks and Psyche smiled cheerfully at Bertie as he looked anxiously at his father.

"I'm pleased to see you again," Psyche said when he bowed over her hand. "May I present Miss Rivers—Miss Rivers, this is my brother's friend, Mr. Bertram Garthwaite." Miss Rivers curtsied and smiled timidly.

"You were saying about the pheasant, Bertie?" the squire asked. "No use having a cook that can't cook pheasant when I go through so much trouble catching them."

"Not very good," Bertie said, casting another wary look at Miss Rivers. "Didn't take advantage of the flavor and oversauced it. Then, too, I wonder if he hung it out too long—didn't settle well with me at all."

"Oh, you mustn't hang out pheasant like that, really," Miss Rivers spoke up suddenly. Psyche stared at her. She looked quite animated, her eyes clear of tears, and her brow was creased in concern. "No, the best way is to cover the fresh cleaned pheasant in a pot of wine and set it aside for a few hours, preferably in an ice cellar if you have one."

Bertie looked at Miss Rivers with more interest. "What does that do?"

"It softens the toughest bird, I assure you!" she replied. "I did just that when I was in Spain with my father, and it never spoiled or had any sort of *off* taste. You can roast it after that, or if you wish, make an excellent ragout with the remaining wine in a sauce." She smiled proudly. "And I have never had anyone complain that it caused any ill effect in anyone. Indeed, I believe I have cooked any sort of game you might wish to mention, including wild hares."

Bertie walked over to the sofa and sat next to her. "And have you cooked anything else, Miss Rivers? I am particularly fond of a good beef brisket, and the other day I had a particularly delectable cheesecake from Gunter's."

Miss Rivers looked modestly down at her lap. "My father always loved beef brisket, and he never complained of my special recipe for it or of my cheesecakes. As for Gunter's—" She lifted her chin in a defiant manner. "My father may not have wanted me to mention it in company, for he was gentry-born, you know, but Mama was related to them and taught me more than half of their recipes before she died."

Psyche gazed at Miss Rivers with astonishment. Gone was the weeping, fainting young woman; instead there sat before her one who seemed entirely confident and competent in manner. She looked at Squire Garthwaite who met her gaze with amusement.

"Would you consider staying with us as our cook, Miss Rivers?" the squire asked. "Can't have a cook that doesn't know how to prepare a pheasant, after all."

Miss Rivers glanced at Bertie and blushed. "How kind—I could not wish to impose—but . . . but if you would not mind me trying just for a little while. . . ."

The squire turned to Psyche. "And you, Miss Hathaway—since I cannot allow you to return home in the dead of night, I would be pleased to have you as a guest." He rose and pulled the bell rope. "I think you might like the blue room—it looks out at the gardens. And the yellow room for your brother, as soon as he comes in, which I suspect he will in a few minutes."

"Oh, but I forgot!" Psyche exclaimed. "We need to have Miss Rivers speak to Aimee, so that she will know that Kenneth hasn't betrayed her."

The squire smiled at her. "If Aimee can't trust him without Miss Rivers's testimony, then it would be better that they do not marry at all. But don't worry, she will."

Psyche could not like it that she had come all this way only to find that her efforts were for nothing, but she sighed and smiled and allowed herself to be led to her room. She was well pleased with it, as the squire had said she would be, for it was very prettily decorated and had a large warm fire burning in the fireplace.

"I think I fixed things very well, don't you think?" said a voice very near her ear. Psyche started and gave a little shriek.

"Harry! You odious creature!"

He was wearing his chiton again and his wings waved lazily behind him. He grinned at her. "How can I be odious when I made Kenneth stop being in love with the portrait and helped Miss Rivers get a position here as a cook? I thought you would be grateful."

Psyche sniffed and crossed her arms in front of her. "It was not very good of you to neglect to tell me when you made Kenneth normal again, and I can hardly see that you helped Miss Rivers at all. I was the one who brought her here, after all."

Harry looked a little uncomfortable. "Well, I suppose I was angry at you, which made me forget to tell you. But I did take away the effects of the arrow I shot into Miss Rivers when she stayed with Lieutenant Pargeter—I remember she was a good cook, and thought I'd sting her with a dart—"

"Not when she was looking at Bertie Garthwaite?" Psyche said, alarmed.

"Mmm . . . I suppose I did. Better Bertie than Pargeter."

"Oh, Harry!" Psyche cried. "I cannot help but think it will cause trouble. Not that I think she is an entrapping sort of female, but what if Bertie should fall in love with her—for he might, you know, if she is such an excellent cook. That is the only sort of female with whom he could fall in love, I imagine. And I cannot think that Squire Garthwaite—however much he may be a kind and understanding sort of gentleman—would approve."

Harry wrinkled his brow and rubbed the bridge of his nose thoughtfully. "You mortals do put an enormous number of obstacles in the way of true love. Her father is gentry, after all, and I am sure if they must, they can say she is a widow—everyone knows she followed the drum in Spain, after all."

Psyche looked at him doubtfully. "Hmm . . . I suppose that might work." She brightened. "Between us, I do believe we did quite well, however. And I think—though I know you will say otherwise—I did not do badly when I threw love darts at people in Almack's! Mama told me that Lady Jersey was quite pleased with the outcome— six couples to be wed in the next month!—though she could not quite like their behavior at the time." She paused, and looked at him hopefully. "Do you think I might try it again? Only for practice, and perhaps you could guide my hand at first, just to get me in the way of things."

Harry eyed her warily. "No."

"Please?"

Harry's wings shuddered. "I don't care to be involved with duels again. They are a drain on my energies."

"Oh, but it wouldn't be in Almack's, for I know we won't be going back for the rest of the Season this year. But perhaps you could call upon us at the estate, and we could practice with regular darts. I know we have a dartboard in the attic somewhere." Psyche took Harry's hand in hers and lifted it to her cheek. "Oh, please, Harry!"

Harry looked at her for a long moment, then a mischievous smile grew on his lips. "Are there many assemblies at Tunbridge Wells?"

"Yes, and I know Mama would agree to having me go to them, too."

The clock tolled, and Harry looked at the clock. "It's late, and I should leave you so you may get your rest."

"*Will* you show me how to use the darts?" Psyche asked.

Harry's outline began to shimmer and he grinned at her before he dissolved into a bright glow. "Yes," came his voice near her ear again.

"Thank you, dear friend," Psyche said, and smiled. She felt a soft, warm touch on her cheek, and the glow flew out of the window into the night sky.